The Spanish Jeweller

EUROPEAN TYCOONS
BOOK ONE

LEANNE LOVEGROVE

Dedication

To the picturesque town of Tossa de Mar that captured my heart when I visited. This story is inspired by you.

Chapter One

The captain ordered a Moonlight Margarita.

Next to him, the mature lady with an impressive grey-wave hairstyle, smirked. 'I'll make it simple, dear. I'll have a sangria.'

The female sailor to her left, resplendent in cropped blue denim shorts with a red-striped top matched with a white cap, ordered a gin and tonic.

Silvia Cooke's brain was foggy from the long-haul flight but if anyone had told her that she'd be taking drink orders from nautical characters at a themed birthday party on her first twenty-four hours in the Costa Brava she'd have told them to get real.

It was sort of fun, though. Or strange. Or both.

Having never left Australia before, she was now a world away from her cosy cottage in the country foothills of Samford, on the outskirts of Brisbane. And that's exactly what she wanted. Still, it didn't mean it wasn't all shades of weird. She had been expecting a more cultural experience in Spain, but there was plenty of time for that. Three months to be exact and Silvia planned to enjoy the Mediterranean lifestyle, eat loads of paella and soak up the endless sun.

And get to know the extended family she'd never met.

Only hours earlier she'd arrived in the bustling tourist mecca of Tossa de Mar. Before she'd even had a chance to unpack her suitcase, her cousin, Cruz, had persuaded her to assist at the family restaurant, *Ole Tapas.* According to Cruz, the popular café located on the main strip was short-staffed and he couldn't call on family to help this time.

Of course, she'd help. Silvia brushed off her jetlag and her desire to explore this new and strange town. She owed her cousin. After all, he was putting her up at his place during her extended stay and he was family; the only family she had now. And besides, what better introduction to Tossa de Mar than being thrown in the thick of the local scene?

As she listened to the drink orders, her eyes caught the platter of crab stacks, shrimp canapes, chicken and fish bites and buckets of loaded fries. Urgh. Her stomach roiled. This food was disgusting but perfect for the beach theme of the party. She'd much rather be eating the delicious tapas the restaurant offered. And she would. Silvia vowed to taste each dish before her trip was over.

The captain was speaking to her. Tuning back in, she folded the page over in her notebook and scribbled down the drinks' order; no way could she rely on her tired brain. 'A Moonlight Margarita,' she repeated. Hopefully, the bar staff would be familiar with that concoction.

'It's for my aunt.' The captain loomed over her; his presence was overwhelming but not unwelcome as she inhaled his woody scent.

She imagined cologne wasn't in plentiful supply on whatever ship he'd sailed in on, but it was divine and immediately transported her to the lush rainforests of home. As she smelled pinecones and the freshness that followed a rainfall, a large dose of homesickness arrived.

Already.

A guest bumped into the captain and he bustled forwards, hands outstretched, palms flat, narrowly avoiding her. She faced a snow-white jacket that exaggerated his broad chest. Her head hooked up, unable to take in all of his tall frame. Like the Spanish men around her, he was dark-featured, and like the ocean that lapped at the shore only metres from the restaurant, his eyes were crystal blue.

She swallowed. This Spanish man was ridiculously good-looking in a dark and broody sort of way. He carried the in-charge-of-a-boat persona well.

He could save me in an emergency. Her eyes roamed shamelessly over his body. A white belt hung at his waist with what she presumed was a naval insignia on the buckle. Her dry mouth moistened at the gaping neckline that exposed a curl of dark chest hair.

And his body heat. Their close proximity sent blood coursing through her body. He was so damn attractive, every nerve ending in her body tingled. He could capture her and sail her away on his boat whenever he wanted.

She was on holiday after all; had been single for a long time and deserved to have some fun.

Could I?

Yes, but would I?

Huh! As if...

Silvia didn't need to be rescued by some dude in dress-ups who probably didn't even know how to drive a boat.

People moved away and the captain stepped back. Shaking off whatever had taken over her, Silvia plastered a smile on her face. 'And what are you having then?'

He paused, took another step back and considered her. Her eyes were drawn to his lips as his tongue swiped across them. Until . . . an arm adorned in sparkly bling snaked around his middle. He startled at the touch and his mouth compressed into a thin slash. The movement was like a circuit breaker, crashing Silvia back down to earth once more.

In the dim restaurant, it was easy to miss, but Silvia spotted his stiff stance as the arm clutched his waist. Even the slight upturn and sway of his head gave away his discomfort.

There was a flash of sparkle from the woman's arm. She was dressed as a mermaid with a skimpy string bikini showing off her buxom cleavage, but Silvia gawped at the jewellery. All kudos to the captain who didn't seem to notice anything other than the jewels, too. He grasped the mermaid's arm.

Silvia's gut twisted. A romantic gesture? Was he going to lift the milky white hand to his ravishing lips and kiss the woman's bare skin? He might have but instead, he turned her wrist this way and that, examining the bracelet at each angle.

Hundreds of diamonds surrounded a dozen blood-red rubies on a thick gold chain to support the weight. Each ruby was surrounded with smaller diamonds before linking together.

At each twist, the jewels hit a beam of light and sent dazzling rays in every direction.

Silvia closed her open mouth. Even with her amateur knowledge, the jewellery was nothing short of spectacular. The captain obviously thought so too as he gazed at it intently. Silvia's fingers twirled around her own bracelet, feeling its smooth edges and familiar twists in the gold and the solitary, large gemstone. She wanted to reach out and touch the ruby bracelet too. In better lighting, she could check out the intricate workmanship and quality of the jewels. But even without close examination, she knew it was worth a fortune.

Until now the party had been like a movie with a bunch of bad actors, but in a split second the movie soared from G-rated to James Bond-style X-rated thanks to the perfect sea creature and her expensive jewels.

Oh, and not to forget the handsome captain. Silvia waited for him to smile seductively, sweep the mermaid into his arms, tip her back and claim her lips in a passionate kiss.

All of a sudden, Silvia wanted to be that nautical character.

Instead, the captain frowned and removed her hand from his waist. Not bothered by the rejection, the mermaid battered her lashes at him before leaning in and whispering in his ear.

Why am I still standing here? She'd been caught up in the moment but she had drink orders to fill.

'Sorry, what drink did you want?' she asked the captain again.

'A beer, please.' He tugged at his already loose collar and without a backward glance at the mermaid, walked away.

The woman pouted and watched him stride across the room. 'I'll have a tequila shot, make it a double.'

Okay.

Silvia moved through the crowd and placed the orders at the bar. Cruz rushed past and she pulled him aside. 'Who *are* these people?'

He laughed and shouted Spanish over her head, ordering someone to do something urgently. 'Didn't I tell you?'

'No. You failed to mention that I would be waitressing for a group of adults dressed as their favourite sea creatures!'

'Ah. Sorry, it's been hectic. 'It's the Blanco family.'

'What?" She leaned in further, fighting against the blaring music to hear him. 'These people dressed in these ridiculous costumes are the Blanco family?'

Her cousin nodded.

'You're telling me that they are the world-renowned jewellery family?' She stared back at the crowd. Could this be true? Was it serendipity or a pure fluke? Silvia had travelled across the world to this small town at the request of her grandmother. Part of that request related to *Blanco Fine Jewels* and here they were, less than three metres from her.

'Uh, huh. Exactly. It is the father, Ramon's, signature birthday.'

Both their heads turned in the direction of the private room filled with over fifty guests. All in costume and having a fabulous time drinking and eating. 'Don't tell me, I want to guess which character he is.'

Cruz waited.

'Is he the castaway?'

Cruz smirked and shook his head.

'The crab? The pirate? Maybe one of the lifesavers?'

'No.'

'He's not the captain, is he? He'd be too young?'

'That's his son, the current CEO.'

'The captain? That guy just there?' Silvia pointed.

'Yes. Watch out for him. He's a notorious womaniser, loves everything in a skirt and even better in his jewellery and wearing not much else.'

The barman shouted at Cruz who turned away to listen.

'*Jefe, queja en el frente sobre su comida*!'

'I've got to sort out a dinner complaint,' Cruz spun back to face her. 'Bet they're a Brit!' he shouted as he raced away. Tossa de Mar was a popular holiday destination for the English.

'Wait,' she called after him. 'You didn't tell which one was Ramon?' Her words were swallowed by the cacophony of the dining room.

The barman signalled the drinks order was ready. A thrill raced up her spine despite the ache that formed at her temples. Now she knew who the guests were, she'd take every opportunity to mingle with one of the most famous jewellery families in the world.

Silvia pushed the palms of her hands into her eyes to alleviate the fatigue that was setting in. If she couldn't have tapas, she'd kill for a banana right now.

Collecting the tray, she headed to the function room. Timber tables and chairs, and photos of the local town lined the walls. Helium balloons in various shades of metallic glory floated at the ceiling. A fish chatted to a dolphin and Neptune spoke to a clam.

The captain was at the furthest reach of the room in the corner, scrolling through his phone. Silvia marched over intending to drop the bottled beer on his table and scat. Instead, her steps slowed as she admired him. He stood tall; one ankle crossed over the over in what should have been a relaxed stance but his body was stiff. Against all force of her will, her stomach performed a funny little flip as she approached

Damn this guy.

He was the definition of hot in every language. He must know it too. A bit of an intimidating "too cool for school" vibe. And she sensed that's exactly how he liked it.

She placed the bottle upon a coaster. As she moved away a hand gripped her wrist. Was this his signature move? Had anyone told him it wasn't a turn-on?

His fingers were warm upon her skin. She glanced down and realised he was examining her bracelet. Okay, made sense given the man was a jewellery connoisseur, gems and jewels were his thing. But did he examine every piece of jewellery on every woman he encountered?

As he lifted her arm closer to his face his warm breath caressed her skin causing a succession of more dips and dives to her insides. But his grip was too tight and she tried to pull her hand away.

'Where did you get this?'

'What? Why?'

'Where are you from?' He shot the questions at her in English.

Heat crawled up Silvia's neck. She tugged her arm away again but bloody hell, he wasn't letting go. The attraction of moments ago vanished. Her jaw clenched and it was on the tip of her tongue to tell him to bugger off.

'Australia,' she said keeping the sneer out of her voice.

'Australia?' he repeated.

'Yes, why?'

At that moment, a loud rendition of '*Happy Birthday*' burst out of the speakers, and a goldfish carried a giant tower cake alight with candles. The captain's attention diverted and Silvia snatched her arm from his grip and strode from the room.

Chapter Two

The music died away and a raucous rendition of the celebratory song rang out. Arlo mouthed the words and tugged at the edges of his collar. It was already loose so he pulled it harder. Damnit, he was used to wearing a tie. He looked like a buffoon dressed up in this costume but it had been the only outfit he'd been prepared to wear. On the rack, it had looked almost normal with its white jacket and long navy pants. But then there was that ridiculous stiff cap. The whistle hanging from his belt was kind of cool. But now, he'd had enough of playing dress-up and he ripped off the jacket and hung it over the back of the chair. He'd abandoned the hat hours ago. Sea captain, be damned. He'd never enjoyed playing games. Being surrounded by his family parading around as sea creatures was a certain kind of torture.

But this frivolity was the least of his worries.

His mother, Valencia, stood by his father as he blew out the candles. A puff of smoke spiralled towards the ceiling. She smiled at their guests, her hand resting on Ramon's forearm, his father oblivious as he responded to the cheers of family and friends. A picture of true love. Arlo's guts twisted. With the candles out, his father received congratulatory slaps on the back leaving his mother to serve the cake. The other female members of the family lined up to assist.

Arlo followed his father's steps across the room until he paused against a long, narrow and high bench. Somewhere on the short walk, he'd acquired a stout glass. Ramon stopped closely behind a woman, causing her to turn. She wore a short navy dress with white stripes at the hem and a low-cut ruffled collar. High stiletto heels completed the outfit. What was she? Some sort of sailor's mate? Deckhand? Whatever figure she was embodying, his father lapped her up like water on a hot day.

Arlo curled his fists to control the urge to punch that lascivious grin right from his father's face as he leered at the woman. Did the man have no self-respect? Or at the very least respect for his wife?

Turning away, Arlo searched for Valencia. She was facing in the opposite direction as she chatted to her sisters and relatives. He looked back at his father who was now whispering in the woman's ear. One day Arlo might just clock him one, regardless of the consequences.

The pulse in his neck catapulted at an unhealthy speed as he scanned the room. Everyone laughed and was having fun. No one had a care in the world. As much as he hated himself for it, his stomach churned. It wasn't his extended family who had to come up with the next best design to keep this lavish lifestyle in check, it was him, Arlo Blanco who had to be the saviour, the one to ride them to victory.

Usually, he wouldn't break a sweat over responsibility, that was his forte, but where ideas had always flourished like a well-watered garden, his bed was now dry and suffering a drought.

Arlo had not long taken over the company and sales had dipped. Publicly his predecessor father remained optimistic saying things would improve. But privately he blamed the new CEO. This made no sense because his father had trained him, and Arlo hadn't done anything different, in fact, he was more conservative than his flamboyant father. Given the current company status, Ramon was having difficulty handing over control and he'd been over Arlo's shoulder examining each decision and questioning his judgement.

Arlo's hand inched up toward his collar again. He lowered it, stretched out his long fingers, and gripped his beer bottle instead. It would be all right. His father had worked hard his entire life, especially after taking over from *his* father, the founder of *Blanco Fine Jewels*. So, yes, his father might deserve a party to celebrate his birthday. Even if it was a ridiculous shindig. But no one cared for his view.

It hadn't been smooth sailing but Arlo could not contemplate failure. This third-generation family business would not fold on his watch.

Not for the first time he contemplated what the company needed. The answer was always the same: new, innovative, and unique designs. Those not considered or thought of by their competitors in a market that was forever expanding with cheaper and more accessible jewellery. *Blanco Fine Jewels* were the top of the range and only catered for a small percentage of the market that could afford them. That's the way he wanted it to stay: exclusive. But he needed designs that would fly off the shelves despite their price. He needed the most beautiful jewellery anyone had ever seen.

The Australian waitress glided through the room to serve slices of the seascape cake. It would be easy to mistake her for a local with her dark hair and features and the distinctive mole above her top lip. Her jewellery intrigued him. The style, cut and shape of that bracelet screamed designer. Arlo hadn't gotten a close enough look, but he'd say it also had the very best of gems. It was unique, different. He couldn't place the designer. But more importantly, how was a waitress wearing something of that calibre? And why did it trigger memories?

The noise in the room doubled and older members of the family danced on the shiny timber floor in the corner. The beer bloated his belly when all he wanted was a nice sweet Moscato and to get the hell out of there. Arlo rubbed his hand down his face.

'It's not that bad, is it?'

Adriana Montebello murmured in his ear, her warm breath tickling rather than tantalising. A former flame, he was surprised his mother had invited her. Ever since he'd been back in Tossa de Mar, his childhood sweetheart had appeared frequently at family dinners.

'Nice costume,' he said, unable to avoid his sarcastic tone. If Adriana aimed to wear as little as possible, she'd succeeded. Dressed as a jellyfish, she wore a micro green bikini top and tulle see-through skirt. It was true, all the beautiful women from the Costa Brava were in the room tonight.

She fluttered her tentacles in response to his comment and broke into a wide smile. No sensuality, thank goodness. He didn't have to pretend. They might have shared their first clumsy kiss, but there was no future for him and Adriana, despite both being at the wrong end of their marriages. If only his mother had received the message. As Arlo glanced across the room, he spied his mama; Valencia lifted her drink in salute and grinned.

The sapphire drop earrings Adriana wore swayed as she took a sip of her drink. He loved those earrings. Arlo leaned in close and fingered them. 'They remain one of our finest designs.'

She swung them again for effect. 'I feel like royalty when I wear them. They sparkle and dazzle everyone I meet. Next on my list is the matching necklace. They are divine together.'

The comment both lifted his spirits and made him feel sick simultaneously. The thought of a five-figure sale of a well-known design would be splendid timing. But to someone they knew? No doubt a heavy discount would be applied and the profit would disappear. If his mother had any say, she'd give the piece away, particularly if she thought it would cement a relationship between him and Adriana.

His mind turned back to jewels. His lifeblood. His one and only passion. He lived and breathed jewels, it was all he thought about. Who had designed the set Adriana wore? They'd had a turnover of skilled design staff in recent years. One of their current problems. Headhunting a major competitor's designer had not worked out well. The designs had been lacklustre and the sales poor. Plus, the designer was American, and the lifestyle of Spain appeared to have little lure. The current recruit was shaping up much better.

Adriana laid her head on his shoulder. Instinctively he lowered his head and rested it on hers, like he would to a sister or friend. He just had to get through the party and then he could sort out the rest of the mess.

———

Yep, another woman hanging off the captain. Cruz was right. This time a jellyfish whispered in his ear; she giggled and he smiled in reply. Admittedly, the manager of *Blanco Fine Jewels* seemed more interested in the jewels that hung at her ears. Again, another fine specimen. Were all the jewels in the room Blanco? Silvia would have to check out their catalogue later. If the accessories on display tonight were the calibre of their range, they fitted the description of *fine.* As perfect as her grandmother had told her. Instinctively she twirled her bracelet once more.

Silvia collected empty glasses from nearby tables. The woman clutched the captain's elbow and dragged him towards the exit. Another notch in the bedpost for the high-flying CEO? Damn, he might be the hottest guy in Tossa de Mar and head honcho of the jewellery business, but she vowed to stay away from him. She'd come to Spain for the summer to lay her grandmother to rest, not to get involved with the town gigolo.

Chapter Three

It took a moment for Silvia to orient herself in the unfamiliar room. Her head was heavy, her mouth was dry and her eyes scratchy after only managing to snatch a few hours' sleep. In other circumstances, it would be a wowser of a hangover, excepting she hadn't had a drink. Clearly, jetlag was not her friend. Opening her eyes now, Silvia was wide awake, any further sleep elusive.

But she was in Spain.

Rolling over, she soaked up the view through the glass bay windows in her bedroom. The world was dim at the young fringes of a new day and the sun was only a bare glimmer on the horizon.

She sat up. The view from Cruz's apartment topped the valley vista from her grandmother's kitchen window at home in Samford. That view was of spectacular verdant rolling hills that encapsulated the valley where she lived. Scattered with gum trees and native wildlife, it was a scene out of a nature book and one people drove hours to see. It always made her breath hitch. Without warning, another wave of homesickness hit.

Samford had green pastures and open spaces. Tossa de Mar had deep blue ocean extending toward the horizon meeting the lighter shade of the sky. If she described her home as green, Silvia would describe this town as blue. The blues faded into the sandy stretch of beach surrounded on one side by the historical old town castle—a castle on a beach! —and the more popular tourist strip to the front and left. If she were an artist or a photographer, she'd capture that scene. Looking at it cleared her head and made her heart sing. What a natural tonic. She pushed aside the homesickness, jumped out of bed and settled for a panoramic shot on her iPhone.

The sun slowly climbed above the horizon and lit the beach making the pebbles and shells shine. She needed to be out there, amongst it, to watch the new day begin. Searching through her unpacked suitcase she found her activewear. Grabbing a few spare coins, she slipped them into the zipper pocket, fetched her mat and headed out the door. Cruz and his housemate, Leo wouldn't be up for hours after the drinks they'd consumed after shift last night.

The obvious place to head was the castle. Silvia wasn't a history buff, but who didn't love an old historic village with a castle complete with a turret and a walled boundary?

She wandered in that direction unfamiliar with the town. Nerves twisted her tummy. What if she got lost? With one turn of her head, she could encompass the entire width of the place, so surely, she couldn't. And what if she did? Repeating the rhetoric to herself, she couldn't deny that fear and excitement flooded through her in equal measure.

The road eventually led to the rear of the old village. The brickwork of the castle was to her left. Silvia walked a few more steps along a narrow path and stumbled upon an idyllic tiny cove. The water was clear as it rushed towards the beach and turquoise before turning the deepest and darkest of blue out in the great ocean. The cove was only a few metres wide and deserted at this time of morning. Stranded on the beach was a well-used wooden dinghy. The sun had risen fully now. The morning sunlight bounced off the surrounding cliff face turning the stone orange. But the beach was protected from the morning sun and provided enticing patches of shade.

A perfect spot for yoga. Quiet, secluded and the scenery meditative itself.

Silvia whipped out the mat, sat down on the sand and inhaled deeply. She relaxed as her fatigue melted away. Yoga had been her saviour. The five years she'd cared for her ailing grandmother was a time of worry and uncertainty about the future. What had started as a way of getting her frail grandmother moving with gentle exercise had evolved into an obsession. She hadn't gone woo-woo but rarely a day passed when she didn't at least perform some quick stretches or deep breathing. A good forty-minute routine was her preference.

Silvia morphed into the zone and performed a pose she'd mastered over the years, the sirsasana headstand. It was hard and she was proud that she could hold it effortlessly. The quiet surrounded her until a repetitive pounding on the pavement interrupted her peace and she opened her eyes. After all, she was alone on a secluded beach in a foreign country.

A few metres to her right, a large mass of black and white shook from side to side. The faintest sprinkle of water reached her, and she blinked. The dog paused for only seconds before bolting at high speed, four legs pumping hard, heading straight for her. With her serenity losing its grip, Silvia wobbled. The dog kept running and behind a man pelted after it. Sand splayed onto her blanket and into her eyes as the dog propelled itself forward. Silvia spat out the sand on her lips as the dog approached, eyes focused on her. The animal was going to see her, right, and veer in the other direction? Her heart accelerated as she lowered her legs to return to earth, but she was too slow. The dog rammed into her torso and sent her sprawling to the ground. She landed with a thwack to her side, her head jerking backwards. The sand that had appeared so soft and idyllic only moments ago was as hard as concrete.

The dog sat at her side, its sizeable paws resting out front while it huffed out big breaths. It sniffed her head and gave her a wet lick. As she moved into a sitting position, the dog sprang back into action and bolted away, flicking up more sand.

A man arrived at her side, his bare chest glistening with sweat. He positioned his hands on his hips, bent over at the waist and blew out breaths so that his cheeks ballooned. Rippled muscles stretched along his arms. The scene reminded her of the old television soft drink commercial featuring a handsome yet sweaty man gulping down a sugary drink after exercise. Suddenly, Silvia was very thirsty.

'I'm so sorry. He's still a puppy and a little uncontrollable…'

'You don't say.' Silvia shaded her eyes with her hand to make out the guy in front of her.

She should have realised immediately by his overbearing presence that took up the available room on the small beach and by his woody smell. A drip of sweat rolled off him and landed on her arm as they stared at each other.

Her heart beat faster.

He recognised her at the same time she recognised him.

Arlo Blanco. CEO.

The captain lifted a finger, insinuating pause. 'Wait here. I'll be back in a minute,' and chased after the runaway dog. It was a useless command because Silvia wasn't going anywhere.

The dog leapt from the beach to the rocky path above and veered away. With impressive agility, the captain closed in on the animal as he yelled in fast Spanish.

Silvia fixated on the captain's long and defined legs as he bounded upwards until his foot caught and he stumbled, landing heavily on the pebbled path. She grimaced watching as the captain lay sprawled, arms outstretched in front of him to soften the blow.

The dog paused and waited to see if his owner was playing a trick and would spring back to life and commence the chase again. When he didn't, the dog whimpered in sympathy and went to his side, nuzzling him with his long, wet tongue. The dog circled. Shit, he must be hurt.

Silvia raced over to check. 'Are you okay?' She knelt at his side, instinctively petting the dog when she should be going crook at him for his naughty behaviour.

Arlo looked up from his prone position and shifted onto his elbows.

'I'm fine. But I'd better invest in some dog training.' He got onto his knees and rose. Blood trickled down both shins. The only other casualty was his palms. He rubbed a few pebbles caught under the skin and winced.

'That'll need a good cleanout,' she said.

'Yes.' He nodded. 'I'm sorry. Are you okay? Gus hit you hard.'

Silvia stretched her torso and reached her arms above her head. 'I'm fine.'

Gus loped around both of them with a stick in his mouth. He dropped it at Arlo's feet and when he ignored him, placed it across Silvia's bare toes.

Laughing, she leaned down, ruffled his ears and patted his body. 'You are adorable but very naughty. Doesn't he have a lead? Might avoid these problems in the future?'

Arlo pulled it from the back of his pants and held it up, grinning. 'Yes, stupid. I thought I'd let him run free. But no more, Gus, until you are trained.' His voice was stern as he clipped on the lead and pulled the dog sharply until he sat.

The muscles of Arlo's chest were clearly defined and wet with sweat. Did he have a shirt tucked back in those shorts too? But why would you cover up a body like that? Silvia licked her lips. She really should have brought some water with her. The day was heating up now and locals were flocking to the beach.

Arlo stretched tall and towered over her. She'd always been short but next to him, she felt like a Smurf.

'You were at the *Ole Tapas Bar* last night, yes?'

She smiled at his broken English. 'Yes, I was, captain.' She saluted and cracked a smile.

He shook his head. 'Ah, no. Let's forget about that. I am Arlo.' He leaned in and kissed her on either cheek. Heat suffused her neck and face. She hoped it wasn't obvious. She was sure she'd get used to this custom, in fact, she liked it, but it felt unusual from strangers. Arlo didn't notice her discomfort as he examined his hands again. They'd probably started to throb.

'I will wash these in the sea, clean away the dirt.' He moved towards the water's edge with Gus held tight on the lead.

'Here, let me hold your dog.' She put out her hand for the lead.

His smile was tight, barely revealing any teeth.

Silvia waited on the shore while Arlo worked deftly, wiping away the blood and shredded skin. From behind he was powerful and well-muscled. All man. The sun glared down upon him and his body shone; she couldn't help but imagine those long, capable arms wrapped around her and his sticky skin from the salt against hers and how it would feel. Her body quivered as he turned.

'Again, I am sorry. May I buy you a coffee to apologise for the misbehaviour of my dog?'

Oh, boy. The inflection of his accent made her stomach swoop.

Goosebumps erupted along her arms. After imagining his body next to hers, his voice was like soft velvet brushing over her skin. But his voice wasn't soft of tone, it was throaty and commanded attention. Arlo Blanco spoke with authority and Silvia guessed most people listened.

But then she remembered. The party, him leaving with a woman. Cruz saying he was a womaniser.

Should she? Why would she? She'd only been here a day. Was it too soon? Too soon for what? She didn't know. But why shouldn't she? There was no intention of tumbling into bed with him. Or worse, falling in love with the Lothario of Tossa de Mar. Having travelled halfway across the world by herself to experience life outside her sheltered existence in the Samford Valley, she could do what she liked, right? Being a big girl, she could deal with the consequences. Besides, she was too smart to fall for his charm.

'Sure, that would be great.'

***

Arlo strode through the familiar cobblestone alleyways and occasionally looked over his shoulder to ensure the gorgeous Australian woman was following. She was a few steps behind, so he slowed, causing Gus to strain at the lead.

The town centre was opening for the day with shop attendants sweeping stoops and placing placards on pavements. He paused at his favourite cafeteria. It'd been open for hours, serving up early morning coffees to locals. Positioned in the back corner of a laneway, it was only a few hundred metres from the beachfront. Tourists rarely found it and Arlo always enjoyed having time away from the many foreign dialects in town. Except for his current guest, of course.

When she reached him, her eyes were wide with childish excitement and she looked around her taking in the detail. Eventually, she focused on him and her face lit up as she smiled. She puffed from the fast pace he'd set and her cheeks were flushed an attractive rosy pink. Under her left arm, she carried a mat. Her tights were black, worn with a simple pale lemon tank top that displayed toned limbs with sculpted muscles in her upper arms. Nothing was left to his imagination. Everything about her was tiny; despite that, she appeared strong. This woman was someone who could look after herself. He tried not to stare, but it was hard.

'I don't know your name.'

'I am Silvia Cooke.'

Arlo gestured towards an outdoor table and for her to sit. 'A Spanish first name but an English surname.'

'Yes. My grandmother is Spanish, she was born here in Tossa de Mar but my mother and I were born in Australia. I've been raised with many Spanish ways.'

He nodded. 'I'll order our coffees.'

The table was small. Arlo moved his legs to the side to avoid their limbs touching. 'You are working at the tapas bar on what you say, a working holiday?'

She shook her head. 'No. It's my cousin's family restaurant. I was helping out.'

He grimaced. 'Yes, not the best example of a fine Spanish celebration but I guess, as you might do at home, my father wanted something different. And a nautical theme was suitable.' He gestured around the beachside town.

Silvia's smile was confident and held his attention. She took off her sports cap and released her hair from the confines of a ponytail and tumbling locks cascaded to her almost bare shoulders. The gesture was erotic but so innocent. With finely structured cheekbones, that distinctive mole and almost black eyes, she could be a European model.

He searched for jewellery but there was none today. Not even a ring. A woman as naturally beautiful as Silvia Cooke didn't need fine jewels. That thought made Arlo pause. It wasn't often he would admit that and he forced himself to look away.

Their coffee arrived and Arlo had a rapid conversation with

the barista. 'Sorry. Silvia this is Giuseppe and he serves the best coffee in town. Giuseppe, this is Silvia, a visitor from Australia.'

Giuseppe kissed her on both cheeks and launched into a story in stilted English about a beautiful young woman he'd fallen in love with years ago from Australia. She'd broken his heart and returned home.

Another customer arrived and Giuseppe excused himself with a smile.

'I thought it was the French who were hopeless romantics.'

'No, you've been watching too many films. We Spanish are very passionate people.'

She stilled, her hands holding her coffee halfway to her mouth. Her lips opened and she stared at him. The air around them crackled with expectation as he held her gaze. Soon enough Silvia sipped her drink and stared into the distance as she returned the cup to the saucer.

'What is this?' She pointed at the drink.

'That is a *café con leche*. The way we drink our coffee. It is espresso with milk.'

'It's delicious. I love it even though I much prefer tea.'

Arlo raised his eyebrow, but she didn't take the bait.

'Don't say that out loud here. Perhaps drink your tea at home. Giuseppe won't serve it; he serves only the best coffee. Don't waste your time in the other cafes. Particularly ones that specialise in *café americano*. That's for the tourists.'

'I'm a tourist.'

'Are you?'

'Well, yes. I'm a visitor.'

'How long are you staying?'

Silvia looked away into the distance as an elderly couple

passed by holding hands. The man pulled a shopping-style cart behind him. 'Three months.'

'Good timing. You won't be here during the crazy summer months. It is incredibly busy in August. This is a popular destination for many people, but especially the English. They love the heat.'

The table wobbled as Gus stood to attention. His leash was secured under the leg of a chair. Across the alley, a cat slinked along the side of the building. Arlo leaned forward to grasp his collar but was too slow. The lightweight timber chair scrapped, slowly at first and then with increased speed. Arlo jumped up, ready to grab the tip of the chair and prevent what he knew was about to happen.

'*Oh, Dios...Gus!*'

The dog sped across the narrow lane. The cat was too smart and scuttled away before disappearing through a low open window about three metres away. Gus stood barking at the base of the sill, keen to follow his target. But then as a bird distracted him, he raced after its shadow as it flew away.

'Gus!' Arlo turned to Silvia. 'I'm sorry for the second time today. I must catch him before he creates havoc with the stall owners and shopkeepers. He's been known to steal fish before. He's not a favourite around here.'

'Okay,' she said laughing.

'Sorry, again. Giuseppe will help with anything you need, *adios.*'

'Thanks for the coffee!' she called out as he chased down his disobedient dog.

Chapter Four

Silvia needn't have worried; it was easy to find her way home. Cruz and Leo were sitting on the balcony sipping espressos when she arrived. Like the bedrooms, the living area opened onto the stunning vista via sliding glass doors so the entire apartment faced the sea. She inhaled the salty air as she stepped out.

'Cruz, you have the most amazing home. This is the best view in town!'

'I know, right? I love it. This view helps a killer hangover, especially after climbing those stairs to get home, it makes you sober up fast.'

Silvia sank down next to them in a comfy outdoor chair. It had been an eventful morning. This was the first time she'd stopped, and had a moment to think, to remember. The yoga had helped until she was knocked for six. But since walking back a shimmer of unease had crept in. She was here, across the world in a different country.

Alone. It was her first day overseas. And the first of many without her grandmother. Was she feeling homesick? In part. It was more a sense of being far removed from her comfort zone in a strange land where everything from the language to the culture and traditions, the food and drink, was new and different. Not only was she attempting to navigate a new country, she was also forging a new future. A life without her grandmother. Paloma was gone.

She blamed Arlo Blanco with his bare chest, blue eyes and serious gaze for setting her on this train of melancholy. Without him, she might have enjoyed her yoga, done a tour of the castle and walked home via the beach. But no, his naughty dog had barrelled her over and their paths had crossed, once more.

Silvia settled her gaze on the distant horizon and watched the white tips surge forward and back. Boats sailed the seas while their crews enjoyed the brilliant weather.

Cruz leaned across and placed his hand on her forearm. 'Yesterday was hectic. Thank you for helping. You saved our skin. Last night was so busy—'

Silvia interrupted. 'I'm happy to help anytime. But where was your family? Were they unavailable?'

Cruz's cheeks went a bright shade of red and he shook his head. 'No, it's awkward. Let me explain. The Garcia family does not like the Blanco family. It is a long-held family feud. I would have been forbidden to accept the party booking but it was worth a lot of money. Their bill was huge!' he exclaimed. 'So, I decided to keep it a secret.'

'Why doesn't your family like them?'

Cruz kept shaking his head. 'Ridiculous argument going

back too many years for me to remember. Not important but I appreciated your help.'

'Your family will find out, right?' Silvia grinned.

'Yes, but it will be a fait accompli and the profits will ease their disappointment.' A self-satisfied smirk crossed his face.

'I am happy to assist, anytime, really. Please just let me know.'

'Thank you,' he replied. 'You come in for a meal, anytime, on the house, our shout. I eat there every night so I never cook. You come in tonight and have dinner.'

Silvia nodded. 'That's really kind.' But she knew she'd feel uncomfortable sponging off her family.

'But, more important. I am sorry for the loss of your grandma. Tough hey, you were so close after your mother died.'

Unbidden tears pooled in her eyes and a pressure pushed down on her chest. In the days following her grandmother's death, she'd been a walking zombie unable to feel anything. The fog had lifted as she made plans to travel to Spain as it had given her a focus. She had to carry out her grandmother's dying wish.

Silvia took a few deep breaths and wiped away the tears. 'Thanks, Cruz. I'm so grateful I could head over here and hang with you guys. You're all the family I have now.'

Leo rose from his armchair and came over and hugged Silvia where she sat. Over his shoulder, her eyes rose in question toward her cousin.

He shrugged.

When Leo pulled away, he had tears in his eyes. 'I lost my grandmother last year. Very sad. I make you feel better.' He perched on the two-seater couch next to her with his arm along the backrest. Silvia inched away.

Why did she cringe? Leo was dashingly handsome; tall, dark and broad-shouldered with an earring in his right lobe. Today he wore black leather pants and a ratty white T-shirt with a hole at the seam. He was clean-shaven and his hands soft. Out of nowhere, she compared him to Arlo. Even thinking of him made her heart bang in her chest as if it was going to explode. Leo was nice, but not in the same league.

None of that mattered. She wasn't in town to find love. She lived in Australia for goodness' sake. Spanish blood might run through her veins but she didn't belong here.

Doing her best to ignore Leo, she addressed Cruz. 'We do have to organise to scatter her ashes. That should be a family event, yeah?'

'Absolutely. Did she give direction on how she wanted it carried out?'

Leo's hand moved to her thigh. Silvia stared at it for a heartbeat and then pushed it away. 'Um, no. She only directed that her ashes should be scattered in her hometown. And I promised her that I would do whatever it took to make that happen.'

'We have a family lunch every Sunday. We can talk about it then and make some arrangements. You'll come, won't you?'

'Yes, I'd love to'

'We always meet at noon. Get ready for a long afternoon. The family will want to know every detail about you and in return, they'll tell you the entire history of the Garcia clan from the moment your grandmother left until the present day! It will be stimulating.'

Silvia's heart swelled at the thought. 'Honestly, I'm excited. I've never been to a family lunch. When you only have your mother and grandparents, it hardly counts as a grand celebration when you get together.'

Cruz sobered. 'Yes, true. I usually complain about my over-the-top family but I can't imagine not having them. You always have a friend and enemy too.' He laughed. 'We welcome you, Silvia, you're one of us now.'

Their hands entwined and he squeezed hard in solidarity.

Cruz was only twenty but he was gentle and kind and was treating her like a sister. He'd said Arlo was dangerous but Arlo had been kind, too. Her last boyfriend, Eddie, was nice but he'd refused to hang around while she cared for her grandmother. It was difficult to maintain a relationship when you couldn't go out on a Saturday night because Paloma couldn't be left alone. So, perhaps fair enough, he'd moved on.

If Silvia hadn't talked with Cruz over Skype the previous few years, she'd have been terrified of him. Both ear lobes were pierced five times and he had a nose ring. His already dark hair was dyed a harsh, almost blue-black but cut extra short. Last night he'd worn eyeliner that twirled at the edges of his eyes. She admired it and wouldn't have a clue how to apply it so beautifully. There had to be a name for him and the way he dressed: nemo or gothic or some such thing. She was out of touch.

It was a fantastic lesson not to stereotype based on looks. Cruz's personality was not harsh like his appearance. How would she judge Arlo? But she couldn't, because she didn't even know him.

Cruz asked a question and brought her back to earth. 'What are you doing today?'

Silvia shrugged and Leo cleared his throat. 'We can't leave

our cousin alone on her first day in Tossa de Mar. Let's have lunch.'

Silvia noticed the use of the word *our*.

'I promised Vincenzo that I'd have a look at his car. His old vehicle needs work.'

'I'll meet you, Silvia.' Leo turned in the seat and faced her, clasped both of her hands in his. They were warm and clammy and the intensity of his stare made her uncomfortable.

Leo continued as if she'd agreed and provided details for a place to meet that he assured her was *delicioso.*

Cruz kissed the top of her head and said he'd see her later.

First up, she'd have a shower and then figure out how she was going to get out of lunch with Leo.

Freshened up and not wanting to spend any more time indoors, Silvia shut the door behind her and went exploring. She didn't see the castle this morning and still had the other parts of town to discover, even the beach. There was at least a couple of hours before lunch. She shuddered but vowed to worry about that later.

Outside the sun shone brightly like at home and the sky was cloudless and blue. It was warm and she slipped off her light cardigan and tied it around her waist. The sadness she'd carried for so long lightened with each step. This place was paradise.

Before long she hit the congested narrow streets with quaint tourist shops selling trinkets and mementoes of painted shells, beach towels, blow-up pool toys and snow globes. There were many cafes selling food with aromas swirling into the streets. Her tummy rumbled.

Silvia stopped at a hole-in-the-wall bakery where the scent of cinnamon was overwhelming. No churros, perhaps Spain was too sophisticated for that. Instead she spied a small, delicate cupcake. A syrupy glaze covered the surface instead of the rich or overdone icing she was used to eating in Australia.

She ordered one and the lady confirmed it was a Magdalena. Such an exquisite name for a cake! The first bite and she drooled. Light and fluffy and sweet and lemony. Divine. Her perfect introduction to Spanish food.

Wiping the crumbs from the edges of her mouth, she continued walking, happy to lose herself in the twisting lanes.

Then she pulled up sharp.

Blanco Fine Jewels. The red swirly wording on the sign jumped out at her. It hung high above the stoop of the shopfront. It couldn't be . . . and yet Paloma had told her that the very first premises were established in Tossa de Mar and had functioned as a workshop, store and sales room. It was where her grandmother's memories originated. It still existed?

Like most jewellery shops it had two glass windows spanning each side of the entry. A striped, red canvas awning shaded customers as they admired the wares. Immediately her hand went to her wrist. It was bare. Damn it, she'd forgotten to wear her jewellery. She felt her ears too, just in case, but the set was missing. She'd left it by the side of her bed and forgotten to replace it. She felt its absence keenly.

Silvia forgot about her gems as she gazed in the first window that displayed sparkling diamonds and other coloured gems radiating their brilliance. The gold and silver bands shimmered. A thrill ran up her spine while her fingers itched to touch the fili-grees, curves, and inlays on the jewellery. Confronted by the precious jewels, she remembered how much she'd enjoyed sketching designs with Paloma. They'd had such fun afternoons in the cosy cottage before her grandmother would grow tired. They'd tried to create the greatest, most elaborate, grandiose designs ever—clearly meant for a queen—and then chuckled at the simplicity of some of their ideas, fit only for selling by a child at a flea market.

Silvia curled her fists and locked her jaw as the familiar tide of anguish pummelled through her. Her limbs tightened and her chest constricted. It became hard to breathe but she knew it would pass.

This is where it had all begun for Paloma. And for Silvia, that was overwhelming.

During those long afternoons with her grandmother, Silvia had entertained changing her life-long dream of being an emer-gency doctor into a jewellery designer. Her grandmother's passion had been contagious and sometimes Silvia's designs made her grandmother pause. Tears formed in eyes that became distant and she'd tell her that the designs were beautiful, and special and should be made into a piece of jewellery that someone would adore.

Were they fanciful girlish dreams?

She'd kept them in a special book that she carried every-where and now sat in her suitcase for safekeeping.

Distant memories.

Forgotten dreams.

Another life.

The display contained many baguette-cut diamond pieces

along with bangles, bracelets, necklaces and earrings, both studs and impressive drop pieces. None of the pieces set her heart racing. Nonetheless, the pieces were impressive by size alone.

Silvia wandered to the next window and drew in her breath at the set on display. A lone black mannequin housed a delicate antique design. The size and intricacy drew her in immediately but the necklace was a fine maze of detail. In the middle, sitting at the apex of a woman's throat was a sizeable diamond, clear and well-cut. From it emanated smaller bead-like gems in long slim chains alternating with flower-like curves. Almost hidden amongst it were pearls of varying shapes. It could easily be mistaken for a lace collar. On the mannequin's ears were the matching earrings.

It was stunning and so was the price tag. So expensive, Silvia imagined even the glitterati of the Mediterranean would think twice.

In her mind, she pictured the exquisite black and gold spinal pieces from her grandmother. Biased yes, but they demonstrated true elegance, and were unique. Even Paloma had confessed to not ever seeing anything else like them.

The hypnotism of the jewels wore off. Yes, these pieces were beautiful and any woman would be delighted to be their owner. But for her, they missed that elusive X-factor. It appeared as if the designer was desperate to create a difference so that the shapes became blunt, harsh and overdone. The pieces had lost their femininity and were too bold with large cuts of gold or silver overtaking the originality of the jewels.

She could do better...

A current of breeze caught the edge of a white sheet of paper taped to the outside of the window. She read **WANTED** in large black letters in English. The store required some summer help. **Enquire within.**

Silvia walked in and rubbed her arms, the chilly store cooling her moist skin. It was a pleasant place to escape the heat. She thought of Arlo. His name was exotic like him and a shiver raced through her. Would he walk out and greet her? Walk toward her in a fancy suit with the jacket on, show her his collection, demonstrate his passion for the business? Or other things?

Instead, the store was empty. She swallowed her disappointment like a hard lolly.

In traditional style, two long counters were positioned down each edge of the store with a small entry point in the middle. Glass counters revealed trays of smaller pieces. A lavish gold and black baroque chaise was positioned oddly in the middle of the store, the darkness of the fabric clashed with the white and shiny floor tiles.

A woman strode from out the back, sun-bleached red hair and freckles across her nose.

'Hiya.' She wiped the back of her hand across her mouth. 'Can I help you?'

British.

'I saw your sign about employment.'

Had she? What was she doing? What would the Arlo say?

'Oh, wonderful. I'm going on an extended summer holiday and we need an urgent replacement.'

An idea was forming. Did she really think that she'd laze around this beach town for three months drinking coffee and helping at the restaurant with a bit of sightseeing thrown it? Hell yes, she deserved it. Caring for her grandmother for the last five years had been tough. This was a holiday. But...

Her brain was not connected to her mouth.

'I have a little retail experience in a café. Serving customers and cleaning up, basic food preparation. But I've done some jewellery design, my grandmother taught me.'

Her grandmother's history was intricately woven into this jewellery brand. In those dark days before her death, Paloma had talked of working in the store before she'd met her husband and moved to Australia. Working here, Silvia would feel close to her grandmother once more.

And it was only temporary anyway, right?

'You'll be manning the store. It's not hard. There's a manager but she's virtual like, shared between here and our other closest shop.'

'Should I meet her and attend an interview?' That translated to: should she ask her boss, CEO, Arlo?

The girl smiled, full and bright. 'No, I think you'll be perfect. Given the short notice, I'll recommend you and you can meet the manager on Monday. Can you start then?'

Silvia thought this was a strange job interview, but she sensed the woman was keen to commence her holidays and get the hell out of there.

'So, you'll do it then?' She waited for her reply.

Silvia nodded.

What have I done?

Chapter Five

Margo squealed in the storefront, the sound drifting through the thin walls to Arlo who sat in his workspace at the back. He paused his work. Had they made a significant sale? Did someone buy a substantial piece or pieces? Or were they ordering multiple items or perhaps seeking to commission something original?

It was unlikely and just as quickly as his excitement built, he realised how stupid his reaction had been and the emotion disappeared. When had he become so desperate? As if Margo, their itinerant shop girl, would care less about any of those things. Probably more the case that she'd been speaking to her boyfriend on the phone and he'd said something amusing. It was him, Arlo only, who cared that much.

He released a deep sigh and sat back to observe the workbench. He'd spent a lot of time here recently. And had loved it. It was a comfortable room with simple furniture and no fancy frills.

Hardly impressive compared to HQ in Barcelona with its plush and expensive interior design. But it was here in Tossa de Mar where the business had started and where the true magic happened. The workshop was sentimental to him and despite their new, large office space and factory in the city, he hoped that being here would channel his grandfather and his ingenious designs of years ago. This is where he would create the next best-selling piece of jewellery for *Blanco Fine Jewels*.

As a small boy he'd loved watching his grandfather drawing with his delicate fine strokes, his head bent in concentration, eyes wide and mouth open, often a cigarette burning to ash in a tray nearby. Once satisfied with his outline he'd colour between the lines. He vividly remembered the colour yellow replicating gold. It had seemed so precious. The designs were simpler and times were different now. People were less extravagant, and demands more frequent. Incomes were lower, too, and there was less access to precious gems and metals. Nowadays, customers were hungry for exclusive and unique pieces. The entire market had changed.

Raking his hand through his short hair, Arlo rose and gulped some water before standing over his desk.

Stupid. He'd been pig-headed and short-sighted. It was business sense to be one step ahead, to know the trends before they became popular; he needed to set the trends. Unfortunately, while leading the company, he'd let go of the tight reins and was now paying the price.

Dark thoughts had crept in and clouded his arrogant vision. Didn't help of course, that his father thought the downturn was due to his leadership.

Seeking inspiration, his eyes scanned the bench with its

discarded designs and sheaves of paper. He spied a large book in the corner and smiled. Once, all designs were placed in this book. He picked it up and turned the hardback cover. Now products were computerised and kept in the cloud. This old way of working still brought a smile to his face. There was nothing like holding a book in your hand and seeing the creations in front of you and not on a screen.

He flipped to the back, to the beginning. For pages, he could recite the name of the item, its origins and in most instances, the designer. Fast forwarding into the future, his detail became scant as his father had taken over the company and Arlo had moved into management and away from micro-supervising what they created. His favourite period had been as part of the design team creating timeless pieces. Arlo paused over a few sketches, his breath catching at their beauty; the intricate nature of the design and the dazzling jewels. Some of these were exceptional and he regretted not knowing more about them.

Retrieving his mobile out of his pants pocket, he dictated a memo to have every design catalogue delivered to him. Perhaps the key was to revisit an old favourite. Or even recycle or update previous best-sellers. Or, even better, the previous work might spark a new idea. Yes, reinventing the wheel was an outdated business concept. He'd pour over the entire collection and memorise every piece they'd ever created: each carat, gem, cut and detail. Particularly their sales record. A rush of excitement swept through him. That could be a useful exercise and he couldn't wait to get started.

Of course, he'd come up with something. And, yet there was that nagging voice of doubt that sounded strangely like his father.

Now, Arlo heard another voice, a sweet female sound that was familiar. There was a customer in the store. That cheered him too.

Straining to hear the soft conversation, Arlo kept turning the pages on rote, in a trance. He glanced over one and moved through them until he flipped too fast and turned back. Was that what he thought?

A black gem. He'd meant to look it up after the party but had forgotten. It was like the one he'd seen but was it the same? For the second time in the last few minutes, he ripped out his phone and Google searched to confirm what it was.

Black spinel. Rare. Not popular. Mined with sapphires and rubies.

Jewellery had been made with the rare gem said the internet. However, the commentary opined that most customers preferred the pretty red ruby or blue sapphire over the darker and less attractive black. Yes, he imagined they would. And diamonds, of course.

The collection in the book was beautiful, distinct Blanco. From memory, the bracelet Silvia wore was similar, or were they both just black gems? Arlo turned the thick pages of the book searching for any other glimpse of black but there was none. Nothing else had been made of black spinel. It appeared they'd only ever made one set with this gemstone. That was unusual.

There were drawings of a ring and matching pair of earrings. He flicked through the pages. Had he missed the bracelet? Nothing. Arlo trailed a finger along the spine of the book but it was intact.

The stud earrings were delicate, encased in white gold with

the gem appearing as if to float. It was secured in the middle with a circle of dainty diamonds surrounding it like a collar.

The ring had an additional thin, smaller layer circling the gem before another row of tiny diamonds layered the edge. The band was plain and thick. Sturdy.

Remarkable.

Beautiful.

He might be wrong and the jewellery he compared was nothing alike except for the same gem. A coincidence? If the pieces were Blanco, how on earth did the Australian waitress come to be wearing them?

'Papa? What can you tell me about a set designed years ago with a black spinel gem? I've checked the records and there's very little information about it.'

Ramon Blanco paused with his fork halfway to his mouth, then took a bite of his dinner. It was Friday night and Arlo was eating with his family.

'Can't remember it,' he said and kept eating, head down, eyes diverted.

That's bullshit. His father knew every design and could recite the entire catalogue. Why was his father being cagey?

Arlo glanced at his mother who had placed her cutlery down neatly next to her half-eaten meal. His brothers at the other end of the table were ribbing each other about something, paying no attention. Their respective current girlfriends hadn't joined them tonight. If he knew his brothers, they'd be meeting up later in one of the popular clubs in town. They were fuelling on their mother's good cooking before a big night out.

'I was looking through the old design book today. You know the one where we used to keep a catalogue of everything made, before the electronic records?'

Ramon nodded, still focusing on his food.

'The set I'm thinking of was designed by Carlo but we've never reproduced another one. I'm wondering why. Perhaps it's time?'

The only noise was his brother's chatter. His father chewed his food with great care and his mother wrung her hands together before placing them in her lap. Neither spoke.

He retrieved his phone and held out the captured shots. 'These,' he said.

At least his father had the decency to look. His mother grasped his hand and pulled the phone over in her direction. Arlo didn't miss her audible intake of breath.

'They're beautiful, aren't they?' he said. 'Why haven't we made anything with this gem since the 1960s?'

It was his mother who spoke, her voice a whisper as if she didn't want anyone else to hear. 'Yes, Carlo designed and produced only one set. He was very proud of it. It was quite innovative at the time. People didn't want black gems back then, and maybe they still don't.' His mother shrugged.

'But then they disappeared.' His father took a sip of his deep red Merlot wine.

Arlo leaned forward sure he'd misheard. 'Disappeared? What do you mean?'

His father answered as if he hadn't heard the question. 'I remember him calling the staff together to show off the unusual black gem design. It was shiny and smooth and different. Exotic. He was excited about the prospect of making an exceptional piece with it.

'Father spent many months making those pieces. He was particularly proud of producing something different. But his joy turned to rage when they disappeared. He thought they were his greatest creations. Some of his enjoyment of life disappeared at the time, too. He was heartbroken but he was angry, too.' His father's tone had a hard edge to it like it was distasteful to speak of. Ramon paused, and looked away, across the table and to the view outside the window where the lights in the distance shone over the clifftops of town.

His parents weren't making this easy.

'Where did they go?'

'All I know is what my father told me.'

Another pause. Arlo tried to be patient but the silence went on for too long.

'And that was what exactly?'

'Carlo said the pieces were stolen.'

'And the police investigated? Were they found?'

His mother blinked too many times. Words seemed to form in her mouth but she didn't speak to them.

'He told me very little. These were things we did not speak of.'

Arlo considered his plate, thoughts ricocheting around his mind. He always shied away from his grandfather's less-than-salubrious past, something that could also be said of his father. If his father was alluding to what Arlo thought he was, then he wouldn't say the words. Would never dare in front of his wife.

A shadow of pain etched across his mother's features. If he'd known the simple question was going to cause his mother hurt, he'd never have raised it at the table. He would have cornered his father later, alone. Too late now.

But Ramon continued. 'It was quite a scandal at the time. The pieces disappeared before they could be sold. I don't know what happened to them. Carlo didn't involve the police despite their value.' Ramon who had avoided Arlo's gaze until now, looked at him directly. 'He was outraged of course. After the discovery they were missing, he refused to talk about it ever again and refused to accept designs with that gem. The black spinel became taboo. I witnessed a couple of young, smart designers in our team approach him with such ideas and he'd go ballistic. I knew never to broach the topic. And now, it is accepted we do not work with the black spinel.'

Arlo didn't realise his father was afraid of anything.

'Did he say what he thought happened?'

Valencia picked at non-existent crumbs on the tablecloth.

'He never said.'

His mother jumped in. 'There were rumours at the time, but who knew?' She started to collect dirty plates, making a terrible clatter of crockery.

'It's very odd.'

'Your grandfather would not be challenged. The topic was off limits and therefore no one dared speak of it.'

'It was a long time ago, Arlo. There's nothing to be gained talking of it now.' His mother hovered over him, plates piled high in her hands.

'Well, what if the business can gain from it? You're right, it was a long time ago and the items are beautiful. We can recreate them--'

His father slammed the tabletop so hard that the cutlery clashed.

'No. We will respect my father's wishes.'

'But he's dead!'

His mother made the sign of the cross, prayed to her God and gestured for the housekeeper to take away the plates.

'Hey, I haven't finished that!' His brother, Marcus exclaimed.

'Well, you eat too slow, hurry up.' Valencia clipped him around the ear like he was still twelve years old. 'Dessert is ready.'

'Okay, Mama.'

Arlo glanced at his father. He sat silently at the end, head bent, one hand cradling the stem of his wine glass. The conversation was over.

Ramon was not revealing the whole story. The theft was a terrible thing to have happened but why the secrecy? It would have been a dreadful blow to the business, any business to lose stock of such value. But given it wasn't their fault, why not retaliate with a finer, better design and trump the thief? Come back with a vengeance. That's what he would have done. He would have fought back. Instead, his notoriously difficult grandfather had given in. That was not the grandfather he remembered, nor the grandfather everyone talked about with fear.

Was this another great idea squashed? Another route blocked for him to save the business because of a family secret? Arlo might not be able to talk to his father about it, but he wanted more information. Uncovering the mystery might mean he could create the beauty of those pieces once again. It was worth a shot. But the conversation left him hollow because if it meant revealing a secret love affair, he wouldn't shame his family.

He didn't want to talk of his grandfather's adulterous ways either or reveal that perhaps the generations of Blanco men might be tainted with the same brush.

But if he could find out more without embarrassing his mother and grandmother well, that was different . . .

Valencia plonked a large serving of flan in front of him. He groaned inwardly despite loving his mother's egg-baked dessert. He knew she'd be hurt if he resisted. His mother and food were formidable forces; he only wished she could be like that in other parts of her life. Valencia often lamented cooking was the only thing she was good at. Arlo had always thought she was the only person able to manage their father. Like Arlo's current ability to manage the company, his appetite disappeared, just like those jewels all those years ago.

He picked up his spoon and ate a large mouthful. 'It's delicious, mama.'

His mother's happiness was worth it.

Chapter Six

'I loved your grandmother. She was my big sister. One day she was at home plaiting my hair, the next she was gone. I missed her terribly.' Tears rolled down Esmeralda's wide and creased cheeks.

Paloma's sister blotted at her face with a crumpled tissue. 'But,' Esmeralda Garcia said reaching out and gripping her arm, 'we have you!'

Sitting at Sunday lunch with the extended clan for the first time was both overwhelming and joyful in equal measure.

For starters, she wasn't used to sharing her grandmother. Without family in Australia, Silvia had only ever thought of Paloma and Joe as hers. But she'd been wrong, Paloma had a family that had loved her.

Silvia couldn't imagine what it would have been like growing up in Spain. They were close; Cruz argued too close, sometimes cloying. Catalina and Fred, his parents, hosted lunch every week. Sebastiano was there too, her grandmother's older brother. He was a quiet man who sat in the corner smoking.

She was out of her depth, navigating family dynamics seemed to be quite an art. Everyone spoke at once, wanted her to answer their questions, to hear her talk about life Down Under, her medical studies, talk of her grandmother and Joe, her grandfather, and everything in between. When they didn't ask questions, they told stories about Paloma's antics as a young woman. Her mind was spinning.

Silvia thought she knew all that mattered about Paloma but she'd never paid attention to her life before she moved to Australia. Before she fell in love with Joe. Paloma sometimes spoke of her siblings, there were five in total, but they were tales that a young child wasn't interested in. Now that Paloma was gone, Silvia wished she'd asked more questions.

After the entire clan was seated at the long oblong table, Silvia announced, 'I've gotten a job in the jewellery store in town. I start next week.'

The room fell silent with the only noise the slight hum of passing traffic.

Catalina broke the silence. 'I thought you were on holiday. Why do you need to work? Do you need money? The family can help you.' There were shouts of agreement and offers of assistance.

'Do you mean the Blanco store?' asked Savannah, one of Esmeralda's granddaughters.

That would have been obvious, Silvia thought. She hadn't seen any other jewellers. She nodded. 'Yes.'

'Oh, boy!' young Emilia's eyes went round. 'No one

associates with the Blanco's,' she said and served herself some salad.

'Um, I don't need money, but that store is where Paloma worked. She talked about it a lot in the last few years…it was her last connection with her home.'

'Bah,' spat Sebastiano. 'Her connection was her family who stayed here. Who went on to raise their families here and forge lives in our homeland.'

Everyone spoke at once:

'That store stole our sister…'

'Our mother was devastated when Paloma left…'

'Paloma changed the day she started work there…'

'It's a long-standing rule that we don't talk to or about the Blanco family. Sort of like a Romeo and Juliet style family feud…'

'I don't understand,' Silvia spoke after they'd quietened down. 'Granny loved that business and talked about it often when we made jewellery together. It was something special we shared in her later years when I cared for her. We spent many afternoons designing creations and chatting about how she learned to craft jewellery. I got the impression that she missed it and regretted never following her passion for jewellery after she left Spain.'

'Her passion for jewellery?' they questioned.

'Did she work in jewels when she went to Australia?'

'She briefly worked in a retail store before she had my mother. They were called Wallace Bishop and made and sold jewellery. She commented it was never the same. And from what little I know about Blanco, they seem to produce high-end jewellery. The shop in Australia was more mainstream and more affordable for people. I don't think she loved it and when she had my mother, she stopped working and cared for her. My grandfather worked long hours so she needed to be home with the baby.'

Everyone paused in thought and the silence was deafening. After a moment's grace, they were back at it, tossing around insults about the Blanco family and how they were to blame for tearing their families apart.

'Granny left because she fell in love with Joe and followed him to Australia…' Silvia's words trailed off and the family watched her and listened.

'Yes, Silvia, but we say there's more to that story.' Esmeralda and Sebastiano clutched hands.

Sebastiano continued where Esmeralda left off. 'When she met Joe, she'd been working at the jewellery store for twelve months. Maybe more. Paloma, like all of us children, was desperate to escape our family hotel business. We hated it. That escape for Paloma was working in the shop. She started as a simple assistant but quickly became more invested in the business. It didn't make sense to the rest of us. She started early, stayed late, and took an interest in all facets of the company. At that time, it was the first and only store of its kind. Not long after they expanded across Spain and are now very successful.'

His face screwed up as if the words were bitter off his tongue.

'We don't know, do we, Es, but one moment she was loving her work, even doing some designing, and then she meets Joe, a visiting Australian, falls in love and is gone, having followed him to Australia. None of it made sense. It was too soon. She loved us, loved her job; our parents tried to prevent her from leaving, but she was always headstrong.'

Silvia smiled. Yes, Paloma was confident and strong. Not so much in her last days. Frail would be some of her last memories of her grandmother.

Silvia fiddled with her bracelet, touched her lobes where the earrings sat and then twirled the ring on her finger. The jewellery was special to Paloma and their touch brought Silvia comfort. She spoke with passion about jewellery and had passed that on to her these last few years. The frailer she became, the more she spoke of Blanco. Something it appeared her family wasn't aware of.

'There was no convincing her otherwise. She left. It was an escape. We don't know if it was an escape from our parents, their business or something else. She was running from something. And why give up the job she loved so much? Why leave her family?'

Heartache was written across the sibling's faces. Pain, still so real and raw. Having met and spent time with the extended family, it made sense now. They were close, had always been close and Paloma had severed that.

'True love?' Silvia questioned. She wanted to believe that very much. Did believe it after conversations with her grandmother over the years. She had loved Joe.

No one commented.

'Why did she never come back and visit us, her family?' Seb asked. 'We begged her to but she refused.'

'I know things weren't easy. After my mother was born, they only had one income and Joe was always at the hospital. Granny was devoted to my mother. Perhaps she didn't want to leave her? Or maybe they couldn't afford it? I don't know. But I do know after my mother died, life for Granny was different. She was devasted at the loss of her only child and then she had to care for me as a little five-year-old when she should have been relaxing in her twilight years. I'm really grateful that she raised me, I owe her everything.' Silvia's last words caught on a sob.

Everyone jumped from their seats and rushed forward to engulf her in the largest group hug she'd ever had. Suffocating, she had to force them away.

Esmeralda held her hand now. 'We loved her and missed her. Our children and grandchildren love the aunt and great-aunt they never knew.'

'It's so wonderful to meet you all, but I'm here because her last wish was for her ashes to be scattered in her hometown.' Silvia looked at her grandmother's siblings to reinforce that Paloma did think of Tossa de Mar as her home, despite the passage of time and everything that had happened. 'Most of her ashes are with Joe in the cemetery in Samford, but she wanted some thrown here. It was important to her. I promised.'

'Where did she want them scattered?' Silvia thought it was Jose who asked, another of Joseph's children, Esmeralda's grandson.

'She didn't specify. What does everyone think? It should be a family celebration.'

Ideas were bounced around, some of them traditional, others more unusual.

The cemetery in town.

Esmeralda's rose garden.

The historic castle.

The cove.

The beach.

'Paloma hated the beach!' Silvia laughed, but the family

expressed surprise. 'Well, she did when I was growing up. Refused to take me there. Hated the sensation of the wet granules between her toes she said. Wouldn't even get in the sandpit with me.'

Esmeralda and Sebastiano bowed their heads, their faces sullen and sad. Such a lot they didn't know about their big sister who went away all those years ago.

Someone suggested a boat out at sea, looking back toward the town. The wind might pick up and blow the waves with the ashes toward the shore of the town she had loved the most.

'That's a brilliant idea. She might have hated the beach but she loved the water. Loved swimming and feeding the ducks in the pond near our home. She found watching the waves calming and meditative. She'd sit on the grassy shores of our local lake and watch me swim for hours. It's perfect.'

In between eating traditional paella and drinking lots of alcohol, the family made plans. None of them owned a boat but could hire one. Cruz would arrange it. They agreed on next weekend, while the weather wasn't too hot before the humidity of summer struck. Before the town was inundated with summer tourists and the life of the town as they knew it, changed.

Next Sunday it was. She would farewell her grandmother for the last time. Her former life in Spain might be shrouded in mystery, but Silvia knew Granny loved this town and her family very much.

Chapter Seven

S ilvia had examined every piece in the shop. She'd wiped down the glass-top counters plus the inside of the windows. Drunk two cups of tea, swept the floor and flicked through an old copy of a Spanish magazine left lying around. Probably by Margo. And only two hours had passed with no customers yet.

Margo had drifted out of the *Blanco Fine Jewels* store with a lopsided wave and on a puff of perfume as soon as the manager, Angelique had arrived. At least she'd turned up, shown some commitment, Silvia mused until she saw Angelique hand her an old-style orange envelope. Her last pay. Margo was off to more exotic climes and her excitement was palpable. Silvia was surprised she didn't run.

Area Manager, Angelique, looked like she belonged on a catwalk showing off the latest catalogue of Blanco jewels as opposed to selling them. Everything about her was blunt: her tone, her neat dress and the black fringe that sat on her forehead in an impeccably straight line. It didn't move even when she spoke.

Angelique performed a cursory handover. As if reading a script, she ran through the ins and outs of being at the shop front providing the bare minimum of information necessary for Silvia to do the job. The register was old-fashioned and still had the till drawer that popped out for change with the fat buttons to push when entering the sale. The EFTPOS machine seemed universal. The same as she'd used in the café at home. It really couldn't be that hard, could it?

Nonetheless, she'd have preferred if Angelique had hung around for a little longer. With no reference checking, and no upper management consultation, Silvia was now in charge of the store on her own.

Conversations from lunch yesterday flittered through her mind. Her family had so heartily objected to her working for the company, so now it felt like she betrayed them, risking the newly formed relationships. There was more to the feuding family tale and she hoped she'd get to the bottom of it. A little pit of anxiety formed in her stomach; she hoped the Garcia family would forgive her.

And yet, on the flip side, she was excited to be in the jewellery store her grandmother had talked about; the place she'd learned her craft. Silvia could hardly believe she was amongst the precious gems.

It had taken time, but slowly Granny's interest in jewellery had become Silvia's passion. With hours to kill each day as her abandoned medical career seemed further out of reach, Silvia had revelled in learning the craft. Now, she had to admit, she was obsessed, too.

It was her grandfather, Joe who'd instilled in her, the dream of being a doctor like him. Silvia had studied hard and got direct entry to medical school after finishing her high school studies. Two years in she'd fallen in love with fellow student, Eddie, and had relished her chosen degree. Until Granny got sick and she gave it away, temporarily she thought. And now, having cared for Paloma for the last five years, she had re-enrolled to continue her studies next semester, upon her return from Spain.

But in the interim, jewellery had taken over her life. And now she felt like the child in the candy store as she eyed off each piece. Which ones had Arlo designed? Thinking of him made her stomach somersault, and threads of dread swirled through her body.

What am I really doing here?

What would CEO, Arlo Blanco, think when he found out? Surely, he never graced this little downtown shop? There'd be more important things to do running the multi-million-dollar company.

Thankfully Angelique had run through the open and close procedures including the solid steel contraption that secured the store. One push of a button and the store shut in on itself, the contents safely locked inside. That gave her comfort. But what happened if she was stuck inside with an intruder?

In a moment of panic, she pulled out each drawer and searched for escape plans and triple 000 numbers. What was the emergency number in Spain? And if she rang, would they understand her rudimentary Spanish?

She needed to calm the hell down.

A couple wandered in, holding hands, smiling and happy. Were they newly engaged? Silvia smiled and asked if she could help. They refused any assistance and did one lap of the rectangular floor, sweeping a glance at the jewels under the glass before walking out.

Okay. Not a busy shop then?

She found a stool on wheels behind one side of the counter and plonked herself down. It slipped on the lino floor under her weight. Gazing out the window, the sun shone and reflected off the cobble pavers. This laneway was sheltered by the other buildings around it and in some places the tiles remained moist from the temperatures overnight.

Across the way was a café. Would the coffee be as good as *Giuseppe's*? Next to it, a florist had a stunning display of flowers in two sets of baskets hanging from low-set windows on either side of the doorway. An assortment of other green stems and red carnations set in timber barrels. The red was vivid and she could almost smell their scent. They sat next to water lilies, roses and geraniums. Next to the florist was a gift store.

Silvia watched people walk the narrow alley en route to the beach. That was where all the action was, apparently. She'd yet to spend any time there. The sandy stretch of cove looked ridiculously crowded most times and was enough reason to stay away in the heat of the day. They mightn't have beaches at Samford, but Australia had some of the best. The beach could wait.

Thinking of home, she had an urge to tell someone of her adventures. Eddie? Definitely not. Amy, the waitress at the café where she'd worked had always been nice and they'd gotten on well. But with her life on hold these last few years, she hadn't kept in contact with friends and she found she had no one to call.

Silvia located a notepad and pencil. While the jewels for sale were mega-expensive, to say she'd been underwhelmed by their design, would be an understatement. She fondled her ring and turned it around her knuckle. It was the only piece of jewellery she wore today. It was too much to wear all three matching pieces together. She had considered it though. What better place to wear fancy jewellery than in a jewellery shop? But if she was to be a representative of Blanco, surely, she needed to wear their jewels?

Her fingers swept across the blank page. With nothing else to do in the empty store, she might as well indulge her passion for creation. Right now, if she could design anything, with money no object, what would she make?

On the plane, she'd seen an advertisement in one of the glossy magazines for a decadent yellow diamond necklace. It had been too busy, too heavy on detail but the yellow diamond was stunning with its vibrant sunshine colour and thickness. It was square and solid and it was this solidity that had appealed to her because it appeared strong and reliable, everlasting.

The doorbell chimed and the store filled with the smell of sandalwood. She scribbled the detail on a chain link before the idea was lost. Pencil in motion, a shadow fell across the page. Silvia looked up with a smile expecting a customer. Instead, Arlo Blanco stood over her. The scent should have given him away.

Oh! So, the CEO would grace the store.

'Where's Margo?'

He didn't let her answer before reaching for her wrist and examining her ring. Then with his other hand, he lifted the paper. Silvia was trapped on the spot.

Heat travelled up her arms until it hit her neck. The flush

continued and warmed her skin. Her pulse accelerated at his touch.

Arlo was back with his typical intimidation tactics.

'She left. I'm the new sales assistant.'

His eyebrows rose to his forehead, his eyes so wide they might pop out of his head.

'You! You are the new sales assistant?'

Was he hard of hearing?

'Yes.' She nodded as she said it to provide extra assurance.

His eyes flicked from her face to her hand and back with speed.

'Have you spoken to Angelique?'

'Yes. She was here this morning and has given me direction.'

He didn't release her hand or the paper. They were caught in an awkward type of embrace.

'You want to work here? Aren't you on holiday?'

'Um, yes. Yes, I'm on holiday but it's three months with nothing to do.'

'Most young people would party all night and then lay on the beach all day until starting over again.'

Silvia tossed her neck sideways to move her long hair over onto her back and stared him straight in the eyes. 'I'm not like other young people.'

He continued to stare as if testing her resolve until Arlo raised the loose piece of paper and held it up to the light.

'Where'd you copy this?'

She emitted a low grumbling sound of annoyance from her throat. 'I drew that and made it up thank you very much.'

He stared at it hard as if it would reveal answers to the questions his mind was asking. 'It's beautiful. Where did you learn to draw jewellery like that?' He examined the intricacies of the image as he asked.

'My grandmother.'

'She was a jeweller?'

'No, but she had a passion for good jewellery. She gave me this ring.'

His eyebrows arched and he raised her hand this time and examined the ring. The size of his masculine, large hand engulfed her small, delicate one. 'She gave you this ring? Where did she get it?'

Silvia shrugged feeling attacked and off-balance and wanting to regain some equilibrium.

'It's extraordinary.'

Silvia's chest puffed up a bit at the compliment. 'It is very sentimental to me. My grandmother gave me a matching set not long before she died. It was precious to her and something she'd treasured her entire lifetime.'

'It matches the bracelet you were wearing the other night. This black spinal gem is exquisite... . . .' His words trailed away and his gaze went to a faraway place before he continued. 'Who was your grandmother?'

The door buzzer chimed and a group of Asian tourists entered carrying large-lensed cameras around their necks that swayed with each step. Despite the warm temperature, the men wore long trousers and shirts with leather shoes and broad hats. The women were in high heels and floral dresses.

Arlo released her hand and headed towards the rear of the store.

Chapter Eight

Arlo took large steps out of the showroom. Once inside his office, he tugged on his collar. The room was stifling. He removed his jacket and placed it over the back of a chair.

Adrenalin rushed through his veins. But it was a heady mix of emotion. His erratic heart thumping too hard in his chest was joy. Happiness at potential sales from the group of Asian tourists. They always spent loads of money. Yes, he was pleased about that.

That topped the list.

But then, Silvia. He wasn't sure if he was able to, but if he put aside his building and unrelenting attraction to her, it could not be a coincidence that she wore a rare, black spinel gem and the only pieces his grandfather had ever made had gone missing and appeared to be identical to those she wore. She liked jewellery, apparently acquired from her grandmother. But more than that, she seemed to have some skill and knowledge in design.

And now, here she was in his store.

Arlo didn't trust people easily but wasn't usually a suspicious man, however, his senses were on high alert. Something wasn't right. Adding to his confusion was his undeniable attraction to the Australian.

But he had zero evidence her jewellery were their missing pieces; it was all circumstantial.

Could he have a spy in his midst? Sounded all Hollywood-movie but he'd heard it happened. People were hired to check out their opposition and garner their secrets. Insiders traded confidential information without permission all the time.

That proposition didn't make sense either, she seemed so innocent and naïve, *nice*. But that of course, is exactly the kind of person his competitors would plant.

He was being crazy. As if they'd place a spy wearing stolen years-old jewellery. Anyone with nous would understand such an act would attract immediate attention.

Okay, not a spy. They weren't in the movies after all.

There was only one thing to do.

He needed to uncover the truth. Was the grandmother's precious jewellery Blanco? Arlo blew out his cheeks. Sixty years after they'd gone missing, those pieces might only be a few metres away. It was insane. Easily solved if he could locate proof of ownership. Each creation came with a trademark number, tiny and inconspicuous on the band or chain. The company also provided a certificate of valuation but he guessed he'd be hard-pressed to get his hands on that. Even though he'd asked, Silvia hadn't seemed to know where her grandmother had acquired the jewellery. It could be the case that she honestly didn't know.

That would presume a level of innocence he wasn't prepared to afford Silvia, just yet.

He hated himself for his clouded judgment. He was not indecisive. Arlo was being distracted by her beauty. Remembering the touch of Silvia's delicate wrist, his mouth went dry. Her fine bones made her seem frail but he knew that wasn't the case. Silvia had a strength about her, an inner fortitude. It was transparent. Obvious. Perhaps as someone who never let people mess with him, he had spotted a kindred spirit. He didn't think she'd let people take advantage of her either or make her do things she didn't want to do.

A feistiness sizzled underneath her sweet exterior. He smiled at her comment about copying the jewellery image. She wasn't happy about that. Yes, gutsy, he liked that. He could imagine pulling her close and kissing her hard on those alluring, moist lips. Hear her murmur in his ear, emit a soft groan of desire.

Arlo could have her eating out of his hand if he wanted. He understood the power of his charm but he wouldn't take advantage of her purely to obtain information. No, he was not like his father and grandfather. That gene stopped with him. But if she wasn't who she said she was, he needed to keep her close. That wouldn't be hard; he'd use his most alluring charm to get a closer look at that jewellery.

The day disappeared as he undertook his endless work of business projections, advertising campaigns and the focus on new ideas. The room grew dim. He tuned in to the sounds from outside, travelling through the shop walls. There were joyous sounds of happy and raised voices as the end of a workday neared: laughter, glasses being clinked in cheers and cheerios being yelled.

Arlo sat back and stretched his neck. He hadn't moved for hours.

Silvia poked her head in. Something inside of him loosened.

'It's closing time. I'll tidy up and shut for the day. Is that okay?'

'Yes. Sure. Did you stop for lunch? I'll always cover for you if you need to grab something.'

'Ah, thanks. I did wander back but you were busy on the phone, so I ate a few biscuits out of the barrel.'

'Oh, I'm sorry. Please interrupt me next time. You can't go without a break.' Pause. 'It's against workplace health and safety.'

'Hmm,' she murmured. 'Do you always work from here? I mean, I understand you're the boss. Don't you have a fancy head office in the city?'

He laughed then stopped abruptly. The answer wasn't simple. How much to say? And why was she asking?

'Our head office is in Barcelona but for the moment, I'm working from here. Circumstances took me away from the city.'

'So, you'll be here every day, then?'

She was insistent.

'Yes.'

Pause. She danced on her toes as she gripped the door frame.

'I'm sorry,' he repeated and checked his watch. 'Given you missed lunch, can I make it up to you...'

Someone entered the store. A broad smile spread across her face and her body turned back toward the floor. A man arrived and approached and landed a kiss on each cheek.

'You ready?' he asked her.

'Yes. I just need to lock up.' Silvia turned back to him. 'Sorry, you were saying?'

Arlo shook his head. 'It was nothing. I hope your first day went well. Thank you.'

This time her smile went in his direction. It wavered, uncertain as if she was unsure how to consider him.

'You've met my cousin, haven't you? He's from the restaurant. You know where you held the party the other night?'

'Cousin?' The guy was young, dressed in black with unattractive piercings across his face. The contrast with Silvia dressed in a simple, colourful summer dress was great.

'We're off to the restaurant. Cruz is working tonight and I'm going to catch some dinner there.' Her voice was silky and smooth, sexy.

Cruz cleared his throat. 'Hey, look, man, did you want to come?'

Silvia did a sharp turn of her head in her cousin's direction. Her wide eyes appealed to him. Clearly, he wasn't wanted. He cast another gaze at her jewellery. He'd have a chance to get a closer look another time.

'No, thank you. I've got plenty of work to do yet. Enjoy your evening.'

Chapter Nine

Silvia was rearranging the lower drawers of the counter when her nose twitched. A deliciously bitter roasted bean aroma wafted in the air and her taste buds salivated. When she stood, a takeaway coffee cup sat on the glass counter. Behind it was Arlo, resplendent in another one of his immaculate dark navy suits that matched his complexion perfectly and hugged him in the right places.

What a way to start the day!

'Did you buy me a coffee?' She grinned.

'Yes.' He didn't return her smile.

'Thank you. Is it a *café con leche*?' She reduced the wattage of her smile from teasing to friendly.

His eyes twinkled. She loved that. For once she understood what it meant when people said a smile reached a person's eyes. If eyes could smile, his were beaming at her. She soaked him up as she took her first sip.

'It is a *café con leche*. We'll have to try you on something different tomorrow. Perhaps a *café solo*.' Now his cheeks creased with the expansion of his grin.

Were they flirting? Yes, duh, of course; they were because he was a womaniser, right? He probably ate women up and threw them out for sport. That's okay, she could look after herself. And why not enjoy herself in the meantime? Flirting was fun.

'I don't mind what you bring me, but aren't you Spanish up with the trend of being environmentally friendly? We should be using recyclable cups.' She admonished him but her tone was light.

Arlo saluted. 'I will remember that next time.' Changing topic, he asked, 'How was your dinner?'

'Dinner? Ah, it was great. I had seafood last night and it was some of the best I've ever had.'

He nodded. 'I love our local seafood. As you can imagine we have good food from the sea.'

'The restaurant is very busy. Particularly with tourists, so after I ate, I helped them out. It's only fair. I'm staying with my cousin for free and eating at their restaurant and not paying my way. I need to contribute.' She shrugged, not sure why she was telling him that.

'I can't vouch for the food at your cousin's restaurant because at my father's party, there was only American cuisine that was well prepared, no doubt, but not my favourite.'

'I understand,' she said. His foot shifted like he wanted to move on, get on with his work. 'Are you busy today?'

The change was perceptible. A slight frown creased his forehead and he stood up straighter, his body stiff. 'Yes. Best get on with it.'

'Thanks again for the café.' Jeez, she would love to know what he did out the back all day.

Thank goodness the morning sped by. The last couple of days had been quiet and Silvia was beginning to think the jewellery shop was a sinking ship. Of course, though, one sale in a day and that would be more than three times her pay. So, she understood traffic into the store didn't have to be huge to make money. And they were only one tiny store in a beachside tourist town.

Tossa de Mar was hustling and bustling and the streets were more congested now than when she'd arrived; it would only grow busier. While the warm summer months must bring tremendous trade, the locals must tire of foreign invaders to their quaint town.

Having only had coffee for breakfast today, by noon she was ravenous so she knocked on the back door, keen for food but also to catch a glimpse of Arlo at work.

'Lunch?'

His head was bowed, deep in thought, a pencil in his hand. At her interruption, his hand stilled and he glanced up. It took a moment for him to orient himself. When he did, he offered her a sultry half-open-lip smile, like he might if he'd woken up next to her in bed.

Ooh!

'Yes, of course. Head out and I'll keep an eye on things here.'

'Would you like something? I can bring it back?'

'Ah, yes. That would be great.'

She laughed. 'Any requests, or ideas of where I should go?' Was he being belligerent or dopey?

'Of course. There's a delicious patisserie on the corner, at the end of the lane. Croissants, baguettes, quiches, rolls etcetera. I'd recommend them. I'll have a chicken and salad roll.' He stood and searched his pockets.

'It's okay. I've got it. See you soon.'

'No,' his voice was commanding. 'I insist.' He patted down his rear pocket checking for a wallet.

Silvia took a step backwards. 'No,' she tried to emulate his tone. 'I insist.' She turned away before he could argue.

Once outside, the bright sun blinded her in a sky so brilliant it both mesmerised her and engulfed her in its grasp. At the end of the lane, the sprawling azure ocean spanned the waterfront, reached up and met the cerulean sky. Silvia found the patisserie by the lengthy queue snaking along the esplanade and into the narrow, cobbled lane to its side. Paloma had told her many things about her hometown but not of its beauty. It was picturesque, quaint and idyllic all rolled into one. It showed off its best weather, too, which certainly helped her fall in love with the seaside village. She smiled all the way back to the store after purchasing their lunch.

'I'm back!' Silvia sang out as she entered.

Arlo wandered out as she placed their food on the counter. Silvia rolled over a chair and sat.

He retrieved a stool from the other side and rolled next to her.

He laughed as he examined what she'd bought.

'What's so funny?'

'Most people are lucky to walk out of that store with any nutritious food and here you are with your salad and fruit!'

'Yes, of course, fruit is my favourite food.' She bit into a pear and groaned. 'Oh, my goodness, this is the sweetest and juiciest pear I've ever tasted!'

'Yes. This is a *Pera de Lleida*, famous for being sweet.'

Silvia polished off the pear before she'd even tried her quinoa and beetroot salad. Next to it sat two bananas and a grapefruit. 'I wasn't sure what you liked so I got enough to share. And there's iced tea.'

'A feast. Thank you.' He passed her a serviette and took one himself.

All was quiet for a moment as they ate and then Arlo opened his mouth as if to say something but Silvia got in first.

'What do you do with Gus when you're working?'

If caught by surprise, he didn't show it. 'He stays at home. He has a nice square patch of grass to roll around on with a strong fence to keep him in so that he cannot get into mischief. However, the small garden in that area of the yard is completely savaged thanks to him.'

'Is that your place or are you renting because you said you usually live in Barcelona?'

'No, it's mine. Because my family live here, I often return anyway so it made sense to have my own home.'

'What's it like? Are you a typical bachelor with a messy apartment, lots of dirty washing and dishes in the sink?' She was joking.

Arlo wasn't. 'My housekeeper keeps it impeccably clean. It's high up on the cliffs and has the most incredible view of the town. You must see it sometime.'

Holy moly! Not only was his voice doing funny things to her stomach, he'd invited her back to his pad!

Arlo was confident, no doubt about that. But he told her this as simply retelling the facts and not in a boastful way.

'Do you have a Lamborghini in the garage?'

'Yes. It is parked next to the Aston Martin, the Mercedes Benz and the Bugatti.' Again, his expression was deadpan.

Silvia coughed and covered her mouth to avoid spraying food. 'Are you serious? You have four cars?'

'Yes, I do. It's a hobby of mine. I like cars.'

'Do you like to race them on the weekend?'

His first smile. It was worth the joking around to be on the receiving end of that grin. He took another bite of his roll before responding. Silvia kept her eyes locked onto those lips. Her stomach dipped and a funny tingle commenced in her groin.

'No, no racing but I do like driving them but not often enough.'

'Why? Because you're always working?'

'It's true. Cars are fun but the business is all-consuming and my passion is jewellery. This business is what I live for.'

A quiver raced up her spine. His words were strong, and forceful, and she felt his passion. And yet she also sensed a sadness.

'It's good to have a passion,' she said.

'What's yours?'

'Medicine?' Silvia shrugged. 'Once I would have answered without hesitation. It was what I lived for. To be like my grand-father. I have always dreamed of becoming an emergency physician.'

'Wow. And now?' he prompted her when she paused.

'And now, I'm not so sure. Five years ago, I dropped out of uni to care for my grandmother after she became ill with osteoporosis and couldn't be left alone.'

'Where was your grandfather? Was he working?'

She shook her head and her hair swung around her shoulders. 'No, he died a few years before. It was only my grandmother and me.'

'What about your parents?'

'There was only ever my mother and she died when I was five. Hit by a car.'

'Oh,' he said, 'I'm sorry. That's a dreadful thing to happen.'

Her eyes misted. 'Anyway,' she croaked and had to clear her throat, 'there was no one else to look after my grandmother and after all she'd done for me, I had to, wanted to. It was my way of thanking her.'

'You must have been close.'

Silvia nodded.

'Did you say she was Spanish?'

'Yep. She was born and lived here until she fell in love with an Australian man and followed him home.'

'I've never been to Australia,' Arlo said.

'Well, that is something you'll have to fix. It's fabulous. Australians are fabulous.'

He wiped his hands on his serviette having finished his lunch. Then he took a big swig of his drink. 'But you were talking about medicine.'

'Not much else to say. I deferred to care for Granny but I never really missed it.' Silvia rolled her chair back and forth with her feet. 'But after this trip, I'm going back. I've enrolled to commence again mid-year. In less than three months.' Silvia stared into the distance, her gaze unfocused. Those words should energise her, and create excitement at the realisation of her dreams being back on track. They didn't.

'You must be very smart. I never attended university, only the university of life. I've always been destined to be part of the family business.'

'But you love it, yes? As you said, it's what you live for?'

'Absolutely.' But there was that shadow again that passed across his face.

A man and a woman entered the store. She was blonde and tanned and not at all Mediterranean. Arlo jumped up immediately, wiped his mouth again of invisible crumbs and went to assist.

They spoke in loud Cockney accents and squealed that they were newly engaged. As a sign of their love, they couldn't stop pawing at each other, their hands and arms entwined and their bodies close. It also explained the woman's rosy cheeks. The man could not take his eyes off his fiancée. He gazed at her with longing and desire, his mouth in a perpetual grin letting her take the lead and explain what sort of rings she admired. Silvia's heart swelled. To be so in love.

Arlo ushered them to the chaise lounge and offered drinks and congratulations. This was clearly his forte. He spoke of cut and clarity and rose-gold and yellow-gold and size and colour, designs and styles. He pulled out trays of rings for them to drool over and answered their questions with certainty and confidence. When a ring didn't suit, he said so. Arlo Blanco wasn't acting passionate; he knew his stuff and she admired him greatly for that as did the customer seated in front of him. Not once did Silvia doubt his sincerity.

She could have watched him all day. She'd only seen passion for jewellery like this once before: her grandmother. Perhaps she had it too? Or if she didn't, she wanted it. Before her was a man with a life-long passion, long-held tradition and boundless knowledge for the work he not only produced but sold as well. She was impressed.

The couple chose one of the selections he offered and with the greatest of care, Arlo cleaned the ring and placed it inside its protective wrapping before it was delicately placed inside their signature purple silk pouch. Tiffany had duck-egg blue boxes which were world-famous; *Blanco Fine Jewels* had delicate and fine light lavender silk pouches with a neat orange drawstring. Silvia had to admit, right now, she wanted one, too.

'Well done,' she said to him when the deal was done, the credit card swiped and the happy couple on their way out.

Arlo only nodded and got back to work.

Chapter Ten

A confident tap on the door and Arlo looked up to see Silvia poke her head around, an impish grin on her face. It was *deju-vu* but at this moment pure lust punched him in the gut. He wanted to smother that smile with his mouth and see those eyes darken with desire.

'That's it for another day,' she said.

He had to drag his eyes away from her lips as they formed the words. What day was it again? What time? His vision was blurry and now that he stopped, an ache penetrated right behind his eyes, throbbing. He rubbed his hands down his face.

What a disaster. Another day and more mediocre ideas.

He'd punched the air with joy after that sale at lunchtime. The happy couple had purchased one of his favourites, and most expensive, Blanco rings with a pink sapphire in a baguette-style setting.

That high didn't last. The prospect of a new idea still eluded him.

Silvia stood at the door, staring at him. If only he could capture her essence into a piece of fine jewellery. Innocent yet seductive; strong yet fragile.

'What are you working on?' Voice like melted chocolate.

'Why?' A frisson of something else passed through him now, his defences upright and sturdy.

Unlike the gilded cage he wrapped himself in, Silvia was an open book, her emotions obvious. She jerked away from the door frame and supported her own weight with feet placed apart, hands on hips. 'Last time I checked it was called being polite and showing interest.'

She was angry.

He had a split second to decide. Alienate or trust her? Keep your enemies close was the game plan, he reminded himself. But the added benefit was that he enjoyed her company, way more than he wanted to, damn it. All with the best interests of the business in mind, of course.

He held up one hand in surrender. 'I'm sorry. It's been a long and unproductive afternoon.'

A slight stoop of her shoulders, a hand on the door again. He released a tiny sigh; he'd rescued the situation. He needed to remain in control and focused.

'I have to, no, well, want to, come up with an original idea. A new collection, something special. Everything feels old and used and anything but extraordinary.'

She took a tiny step forward. 'Don't you have a whole design team to do that?'

'Yes, I do. And they're making some fantastic items in a collection now. But I'm thinking of something dazzling and amazing that will make you catch your breath.'

She peered at him through her lashes and his breath stalled and he coughed to conceal it.

Silvia pushed on, her voice soft and tender. 'I didn't realise you cared that much . . .' but the way she expressed the words indicated she thought the exact opposite. 'Or that you were struggling to come up with new ideas.' He winced as she moved closer. He banqueted on the view.

'I like to design. I've worked my way through each division and understand the intricacies of the business and the important role of each member of staff. For example, if you work at a fast-food place, you don't go straight to the checkout. You flip burgers out the back, deep-fry the chips and work on the production line so that when you are in front of the house, you know the product well and can answer questions from customers. Same concept. My father and I don't agree on a lot, but his approach to training was correct. As a result, I know every aspect of this business.'

'Yes, I observed your impressive sales skills this morning. And it sounds like perfect business sense to me.'

Arlo was aware of Silvia standing next to him. Her body exuded warmth and her scent was of a summer's day, feminine like coconut oil. Her fingernails were unvarnished and neatly trimmed. She wore the black spinel ring on one of her long slender fingers. He couldn't take his eyes off it. It gave him an incredible rush.

Her hands were flat on the workbench and she leaned over him as he remained seated. He felt oddly discombobulated and fought the urge to stand.

Out of the corner of his eye, he searched the ring for detail while Silvia's gaze deliberated over the scattered sheaves of paper on the surface of the workbench. She picked up a couple. 'Wow. You've done all these today? No wonder your brain is fried.'

Yes, he'd been in a frenzy, but quantity didn't equal quality. There were dozens of discarded designs.

None of them good enough.

Silvia raced back into the store. He heard the shudder of the front security door closing, followed by the silence as the world was locked out.

Returning, Silvia held a piece of paper in her hand.

'You know what is popular at the moment? Thick, wide and stunning-coloured gems. I'm loving these yellow diamonds. The colour looks incredible next to white gold, or silver. But I prefer the gold.'

Arlo looked at her scribbling. It was what he'd disturbed her working on yesterday. It looked more impressive today.

'I would love to see this as a centre piece on a necklace,' she said.

Arlo retrieved his pencil and did a quick sketch on the pad in front of him. The sharp square image had struck an idea. His fingers flew across the page. It was a long narrow chain, with smaller square diamonds each ten centimetres or so. At the end, as Silvia suggested, the *piece de resistance*. He imagined it sitting in the dip of a woman's cleavage. He snatched a yellow pencil and coloured it in.

She spoke before he'd finished. 'It's beautiful but overstated. You want it to scream elegance. You want it to allure and most importantly, you want the eye drawn to the most important part. The yellow diamond at the base.' She pointed her finger. 'It's too busy with these coloured diamonds down the chain.

Don't you think?' Silvia pinched the paper off Arlo and held it up, away and in front of them.

Arlo started to protest.

'Imagine a delicate chain but like a bridesmaid, it cannot overtake the main attraction, which is the bride, of course. She needs to be the centre of attention, everyone's focus. The bridesmaids can be beautiful but not more than the bride.'

Damn it, the woman was right. 'Okay. I see what you mean.' He scribbled again and tuned into her presence. But rather than concentrate, all he heard was her breathing, the smell of her scent, her body near his, and his pencil forgot where it needed to go.

'Yes, much better.'

Silvia leaned over and Arlo caught a glimpse of breasts that rose and fell as she spoke. They were small like her and he imagined his fingers fondling them and his tongue . . .

The oxygen was sucked from the cramped room. His body was on fire and he tugged at his collar trying to cool down.

It was too much. His frustration at his lack of success today festered and needed to be released. And Silvia was too close, exuding her innocent beauty and vulnerability yet her underlying strength was obvious as she stood next to him. Who was she to tell him design ideas? But she had, and she'd been right.

His desire bubbled under his skin and his hands itched to wander over her body, feel her curves and caress her skin. Kiss her, taste her. Every inch.

He dropped the pencil and stood, the chair scraping, the sound reverberating in the small space. Locking onto her eyes, he placed his large hand over hers where it still lay on the table.

He felt the edges of the ring. Seconds passed and her chest rose and fell exaggeratedly as she pulled in sharp breaths.

'This is perfect. It's a beautiful necklace and any woman who wore it would feel like a million dollars,' her voice purred.

'You'd look amazing wearing it,' he said and paused. He reached for the base of her neck and traced the curve in her throat where the pendant would lay against her skin. Then he moved onto her bare earlobe. 'Dangling earrings would match it but not too heavy for delicate ears like these.' He leaned in and nipped the pale, soft flesh with his teeth. 'With a bracelet.' He lifted her arm and placed a trail of kisses along the inside of her arm, until he reached her wrist.

'Thank you for your ideas.' His voice was low and deep. 'I'm going to kiss you now.'

Silvia sucked in her breath each time Arlo stroked her skin, powerless to stop it; she didn't want him to stop. Her skin was ablaze and the floor tilted beneath her feet as his lips met hers. He was surprisingly gentle and she closed her eyes and gave in to the sensation of lip upon lip, his teeth nipping at her mouth, his tongue teasing.

It was a burst of taste and Arlo Blanco was exquisite. Silvia leaned in and she felt the taut muscles of his stomach where her hands rested.

The kiss went from gentle and romantic to frantic and sexy in a millisecond. The bag over her shoulder fell to the ground with a thud. She raked her hands through his hair. He nudged her backwards until her back was against the wall all the while kissing her. He placed his hands on the wall beside her head as he caught his breath. Then bit the corner of her lips that were pouted and open for him, reclaimed them, and crushed his mouth against hers, his tongue dipping in and out forcing her to emit a soft groan. Her body came alive as he kissed a trail along her collarbone. The thin spaghetti straps of her dress came away and her shoulders were bare.

Goddamn, the man could kiss.

His mobile trilled from the safety of the desk; going unanswered it danced on the spot. Arlo ignored it but paused, leaning his forehead against hers. Then another sound—her phone, less cranky, less noisy from her handbag, barely discernible. His, however, kept ringing loud and clear.

The spell broke. The room came back into focus and Arlo lifted his hands from the wall and stepped back. Silvia's tongue flicked across her lips and his head tilted sideways, his eyes still simmering with desire. The ringtone of the phone stopped but then it beeped with an incoming message. Arlo straightened, towering over her once more, righted the straps of her dress and tugged down the sleeves of his business shirt.

'That's sure one hell of a way to thank me,' she murmured.

Arlo smiled, tight and thin-lipped.

Her breathing slowly regulated and her simmering desire settled. She balanced on her toes. His hands clawing her hot skin, her insides filled with lust and longing became a memory.

'You can't say I'm not grateful.' His voice was gravelly.

They moved apart and stood side by side.

Realisation hit Silvia quickly. She'd kissed the boss and fallen for the charms of the womaniser! Did she have no self-control? Oh, but she did and the moment he'd touched her lobe, she was a goner. No wonder this man could bed half the town when he kissed like that. His touch was explosive and her skin so hot, it burned for more.

Her family would be furious; she should be running in the other direction. This man was trouble, but she'd witnessed his lack of arrogance and his vulnerability at his defeat. Plus, that passion, not for her, but the jewellery was unbridled. Arlo Blanco was a delicious conundrum.

He picked up his phone and checked the screen. He sighed and his shoulders slumped.

'Guess I'll get going then.' Best to let her head cool.

He nodded and turned away.

Chapter Eleven

S he only gave herself a moment of self-recrimination, no more. She'd done nothing wrong. If the womaniser of Tossa de Mar wanted to kiss her, well she was flattered. And hell, she'd enjoyed it. It had been a shared moment of passion.

Arlo Blanco was a perfectly delicious bad-boy millionaire. At least she knew it.

Okay, Silvia would admit to slight annoyance that she'd been charmed, fallen for the CEO's seduction. But, oh what a kiss! She touched her lips in memory and relived it over and over, going tingly at the sensuousness of it. Who knew kissing could be so intimate, and so damn good?

Right at this moment, she didn't care what his reputation might be.

And if she had the chance, she'd do it again.

Silvia Cooke was a big girl; she could look after herself and was under no illusions about who he was and what she could mean to him. Yeah, pretty much nothing, a good kiss at the right moment. But, Silvia, well, she was on holiday and kissing the handsome jewellery tycoon suited her perfectly.

She could handle her own emotions, what she wasn't prepared for, was his reaction.

For a man with bucket loads of confidence and arrogance—Arlo wore it like aftershave—he avoided her the day after.

That was her take on the situation anyway. Perhaps he was busy, it was a workday after all. But Silvia swore an air of uncertainty clung to Arlo that she'd not detected before. She imagined he was used to women throwing themselves literally at his feet, begging for attention and declaring their undying love. Had she turned him off by not acting that way? Was he expecting drama and histrionics? Or worse, devotion. He was in for a surprise if that was the case.

Arlo hadn't met Silvia Cooke before. There was no chance she was going to bolster his already inflated ego, or goodness, swoon! Even if he was swoon worthy.

But damn it, despite her best intentions, that kiss was all she thought about as he arrived at the store. Her body grew warm and her armpits moist and other places, too. The taste of him, the feel of him clutching her like he couldn't control himself, as if his body had taken over. The deep desire hidden in those eyes that were dark stormy pools. She had felt wanted and desired, even if fleeting.

He entered the store and his gaze zeroed in on her, those eyes staring, not stormy now, but intense and seeking answers to questions he wasn't asking. Without breaking eye contact or his stride, he placed a recyclable coffee cup on the counter, nodded and kept walking to the workshop.

An image of him, naked, out of his business suit flashed across her mind and she was forced to push it away.

Okay, yes, her world might have crashed down around her a little then. The reality hit. Arlo was a Spanish multi-millionaire who lived in a mansion on the cliffs and had four prestige cars. Silvia lived in a simple timber cottage and drove a Datsun. She liked yoga and shopped at her local supermarket. They were all kinds of different. But he'd like her jewellery design.

She tasted the coffee; it was an *Americano*. A smile curled her lips.

Whether it was her erotic hangover or because trade was slow, the day dragged. Arlo's mobile rang dozens of times and she heard his raised voice each time he answered. A couple of men arrived for meetings.

'Lunch?' she poked her head around after knocking at his door. She put on her best innocent face and acted as if they hadn't only yesterday shared a passionate kiss.

He looked up, like seeing her afresh, and shook his head. 'Not today, thank you. Take your time.'

Okay, no repeat of their intimate lunch yesterday. On his instructions, she stayed out, ate on the run as she wandered the streets and soaked up the sun. After all, she was entitled to a break. Let him starve and look after the store. She wasn't his secretary.

Back after lunch, her gaze clocked the window dressings and an idea dawned. She might dust the display, maybe shift around a few pieces, and glam it up a bit.

Silvia collected her favourite sets from the secure trays of jewels and placed them into a creative window feature. She was lost then to a world of blue sapphires. She positioned them one way and then another. Put one in front, another behind. She had to confess; the result was stunning. Their most impressive blue stones were in a bed of dazzling white. She dared any woman to walk past and not be captured by their beauty.

'What are you doing?' The voice was harsh behind her.

Turning, she planted on her broadest smile. 'Ah, so you've ventured out of your cave, have you? Hungry?'

'Something like that.'

'What do you think?' she asked and indicated toward the display.

His head cocked to the side and he pursed his lips like he held in a sigh.

'It's fantastic. You have much more flair for this than Margo.' His smile was fixed on the display.

In the first window, she'd made an elegant show of the blue sapphire jewel. In the second, there sat one piece, striking and alone. The ring she chose was not necessarily the largest but it was the best, in her humble opinion. It had a white gold band with what she guessed was at least 1.5 carats with another large and square-shaped diamond in the middle surrounded on each side by two smaller white gems with yet tinier versions along each edge. To complement the style, the top half of the band also had an inlay of six or so minute diamonds running down each side.

It was a special occasion ring. Silvia knew that any woman— whether she'd been married for twenty years or was newly engaged—could not help but gaze longingly at the piece and imagine slipping it on her finger.

Silvia grew uneasy at his silence. 'I'm new here. But it makes sense to me that if you want people to venture inside and discover what else we have on offer, they must be tempted, right?'

'Perfect sense. Can you do this with the counters, too?'

'Of course.'

'Thank you.' He paused, glanced at her and back to the window. 'I'm out to a meeting. I'll be back soon.' He smiled but his eyes lingered on the black spinel necklace she wore today. Was it because it lay on her decolletage that he had so intimately caressed yesterday?

Arlo returned two hours later while she was busy serving customers. He strode straight to the workroom.

At closing time, she prepared the store and was about to advise him she was off for the evening when he called out for her. 'Silvia?'

'Yep.'

'Come and have a look at this.'

As she entered the back room, he flashed a boyish grin at her. Silvia cursed when it made her tummy perform a funny flip.

Before him, he had four pieces of paper. They were 3D depictions of the yellow diamond. All yellow and sparkly and beautiful. She picked up the ring design. 'Oh my gosh. This is stunning. Just like the necklace you've made the gem the focus. I can't take my eye off it.' Then she picked up the bracelet and earring patterns.

'Do you really like them? Are they original and special enough? I mean yellow diamonds are available anywhere, even though we can, of course, source the best. These designs are not new, but a new take on old ideas.'

Silvia nodded understanding his uncertainty. 'I know, but they're perfect. Any woman would be exhilarated to own one of these pieces. While other designers might be able to manufacture something similar, I think these are bigger, bolder, and brighter. That is to your advantage.'

He nodded. 'Check this out.' He pulled out a mock-up of the necklace, only the pendant part. It was large!

'You made this?'

'Yes,' he answered, his eyebrows lifting in amusement. 'All pieces are made in model form like this before we spend time and money on producing the real thing.'

'Fascinating.' Silvia held it up close to examine it properly. 'Are you going to make the others? Can I help you?'

'Are you serious? You want to?'

'Yes, absolutely.'

Arlo leaned over and kissed her. Caught by surprise, they met at an odd angle and his mouth landed on the corner of her lips.

Silvia turned and faced him, leaning in. Their lips pressed together meeting in unison this time. It was sensual yet sweet and lingered with neither pulling away.

Compared to yesterday's hot kiss that burned her from the inside out, this was softer but way more erotic. And just as good. The slowness, the time-lapse, the placing of his lips perfectly on her. She shifted nearer to him; his lips parted and she snuck in her tongue. He reacted and matched the pressure. A tsunami of emotions and sensations swirled within, and her body tensed, desire thick and strong.

Then her tummy rumbled.

He pulled back, his eyes black ink pools once more. He laughed, the tension releasing.

'Was that your stomach?' he asked but she detected the

sultry tone to his voice. Arlo put his hand to her thigh; it was warm on her bare skin and she wanted to grab it and rake it over her entire body until she writhed. But she didn't move, didn't trust herself and did not touch him back.

'Yes.'

'These designs will take a while. I'll ring Giuseppe and get him to deliver one of his Margherita pizzas to us while we work.'

'He'll do that?'

'Yes. He's done it for me a million times.'

'So, you often work late?' His hand stayed in place.

'Yes.'

'When do you have fun?'

'On the weekend sometimes.'

'I guess you need plenty of time to drive around in your Porsche.'

'I don't own a Porsche.'

He lifted his hand and made the call, gesturing for her to sit while he spoke in Spanish. The words sent thrills racing up her spine and the man was only ordering pizza.

Chapter Twelve

Arlo placed her coffee on the glass counter and reached out to fondle the earrings Silvia wore. 'I love these.'

'I know. You've told me, repeatedly. It's getting a bit weird.' Silvia replied with a smile and a sparkle in her eye.

Arlo ignored the lurch in his stomach and touched the earring at her left lobe, feeling for markings. He needed to get these pieces in his hot little hands, and soon. The constant wondering about whether were they authentic Blanco or a mere replica, was killing him, particularly when he had to gaze at them most days.

'They are beautiful and unusual and I want to know more about them. Can you stay behind again tonight? You can tell me more about them.' His brow creased waiting on her reply and he wished it didn't. He was starting to care too much about the jewels and the woman wearing them.

'I'd love to. I can't wait to keep working. What piece will we move onto next?'

'Earrings? Inspired by these.' He dropped his hand.

'I think you only like me for my jewels,' she joked. Arlo's frown burrowed deeper into his forehead.

He didn't reply but traced one solitary finger down the side of her face.

Silvia placed her hand over his and paused the movement. Her touch caused an electric bolt to race up his arm and he startled. What the . . .? He'd never felt such an unadulterated, visceral reaction before. Did Silvia feel it too? Her face didn't give anything away. Out of nowhere, he felt discombobulated, the room shrinking around him. This moment was too romantic, too intimate and implied too many things. His eyes diverted to the earrings again before he snatched his hand back. Silvia's eyes weren't sparkling now, they were dark and smouldering.

Stay focused. Arlo Blanco did not get distracted. Everything occurred at his command and usually by sheer calculation and manipulation, if necessary. There was no time for steering off course. That had to stop now, today. Upping his game was the objective. He'd get more information about the black spinel gem and they'd keep working on the design of exquisite pieces for his business. The bonus was time in Silvia's company and the only challenge would be to prevent his hands wandering over the soft folds of her skin and being mesmerised by her Australian twang.

Tonight would be all business.

With that goal in mind, Arlo maintained eye contact while he lifted her hand and kissed her soft and delicate skin there. He savoured her taste and her smell as if he needed both to get through the day.

The spring in his step and the resurgence of his enthusiasm as he headed to his desk was about the prospect of the shiny new idea. It was not about Silvia Cooke. Either way, he'd be counting the minutes until closing time.

———

One minute after six, Silvia plonked herself down on the seat next to him. He didn't look up. 'I'll just finish this and we'll get started.'

'Okay,' she murmured and got out her phone and scrolled. 'Oh,' she said a few seconds later.

Arlo glanced over. 'Is everything okay?'

'Ah, yeah, sure. My return flight has changed. Nothing major.'

'Your flight to Australia? You don't return for a long time, yes?'

Clicking the phone off, she placed it face down on the desk. 'Um, I've been here a few weeks now, so in two and a half months, I guess. I'm sure the time will fly.'

Two and a half months.

His hands paused what they were doing before he gathered up the work in front of him. 'I've been thinking about these designs all day.'

Silvia laughed. 'You sure are a man passionate about jewellery. It's an oxymoron.'

'Did you call me a moron?'

'What? No! I didn't call you a moron. I said oxymoron. Meaning that you are a contradiction.'

'Oh, well that's just a fancy word for moron, isn't it?'

'No!' Silvia mock-punched him. She laughed but then the

sound stopped just as quickly, her eyes flickering back to the spot. 'Wow. You have very strong, um, biceps.'

Arlo flexed both arms. 'These strong arms allow me to make fabulous jewellery.'

'You've never shown me anything that you've made. Can I see some?'

Silvia leaned in closer, her laughter lines fading as her expression grew serious. That look, it seared into him, pinned him to the spot. Arlo needed to avoid her, but the chances of that were slim. She was like a drug. In her proximity, his body set off a physiological reaction, something he had little control over; he both loved it and loathed it. Loved it because he came alive, felt something, felt a lot, too much. Loathed it because when it occurred, he lost complete focus and his thoughts were overtaken by her: her smell, her beauty, oh, and of course, her jewellery.

'You would look amazing wearing the jewels I've designed for *Blanco*. No one would know you aren't Mediterranean.'

'Do you like Mediterranean women or do you prefer blondes?'

He wanted to reach out and touch her hair, twirl the strands through his fingers, but he didn't. 'Will you wear our jewels one day for a special occasion?'

'What, for a show you mean?'

He didn't. He meant to wear them for him and perhaps with nothing else. 'Maybe. Or out one evening. We can go somewhere special and you can choose a set to wear.'

Her face lit up. 'That would be awesome. But you didn't answer my question. What is your type?'

He paused taking a moment to reflect on what he was doing.

And perhaps for the first time ever, the answer didn't come to him. On one hand, he needed answers about the jewels she wore, but on the other, he needed her creative input. Or was that simply becoming an excuse to spend time with this exotic alluring woman who had passion, and even the talent, for design?

He balled his hands into fists. The truth was he needed her. So therein lay the answer. What he wasn't yet sure of was how far was he prepared to go.

'How about we take what we need to work with and head out for dinner? I can take you to my favourite place. Seafood, good wine. Spectacular views.'

'I'd love that. I haven't eaten anywhere but my cousin's restaurant.'

He gathered up the paraphernalia they'd require to work on the earrings.

Outside, he reached for her hand and walked at her pace through the winding, narrow streets. Locals and tourists alike were enjoying the town's nightlife. The sun was slowly setting and like most European cities, the crowds starting to build after dusk.

They came out at the end of the path, near the beach. The castle on the right was illuminated, each sandstone rock glowing golden. He paused, and turned to Silvia, giving her an opportunity to take in the scene. Even as a local, he'd never tired of the sight. The size, the structure, and the enormity of the castle, never ceased to take his breath away. Particularly at night.

'It is so beautiful,' she said as her gaze roamed over its contours.

'We're going to a restaurant that sits at the base, along that bottom edge. To our right will be the fairy-tale castle and to our left will be the sea.'

'This place is gorgeous. It must have been wonderful to grow up here. Beaches, water, history.'

'Yes. But I guess as a child you never appreciate those things. I do now, though. This old part of town remains my favourite. And the coves. They are special. Like the one where we met that morning. It's one of our finest.'

Silvia agreed.

Seated, he ordered for them and a bottle of white wine was delivered without fuss.

'You didn't show me the jewels you designed. Can you do that tomorrow?'

'Ah, yes, there's only a select few. As I explained, I only worked in that division for a few months. There was only time for two or three sets given the amount of work that goes into designing and producing them. But I have been involved in every piece since.'

'You know the entire collection off by heart?'

'Mostly, yes, that's my job.'

'You're very good at it.'

Silvia finished her first glass of wine and he immediately poured her another.

'Why are these pieces special?' He pointed to her ears.

'They were a special gift to my granny. She thought they were the most beautiful items she'd ever seen. But now that I think about it, I'm not exactly sure why, but I do know she treasured the set. I wish I could ask.' Silvia went silent.

'What did she tell you?'

'Like I've already said. They were her most precious and trea-sured belongings. But she never wore them, not that I can recall anyway. That's strange, isn't it? I wear them now to be close to her and because she loved them so much. I love them, too.'

'When did you learn about them?'

'Not until I was caring for her; after she became ill. When it was just the two of us and we talked endlessly about jewellery, these and others, about Blanco.'

'Blanco?' The hairs on his neck stood to attention.

'Yes. Many of her memories seemed to be mixed up with *Blanco Fine Jewels*.'

Arlo sat up straight and sipped his wine. 'What do you mean?'

'Well, when she was young, she worked in the store, sort of like I am, I guess. That's why I wanted the position. To retrace her footsteps, follow her path. Is that crazy?'

'No, not crazy at all. Sentimental, yes. But, hang on, you never told me your grandmother worked in the store, did you? Or had any connection to Blanco?'

Silvia looked out across the water. Small ripples of waves washed against the shore silently.

'I mentioned it to Margo and Angelique, I think. Since arriv-ing, I've learned a lot about my grandmother. My memories and those of my family are different. Sometimes, I'm not sure we're talking about the same person.'

'You've definitely talked about your Spanish grandmother with a love of jewellery and these special pieces but I'd remember if you'd said she worked at my store.'

'Sorry, Arlo, it hasn't come up and we haven't really talked that much. I was more worried about how you'd react to me being employed in your store.'

That made two of them.

'Did your grandmother design and make these pieces?'

'Um, she talked with intimate knowledge of their production but, design, I don't think so and she definitely didn't make them. How would she? She knew about jewellery though and that's why we mucked around at home making rudimentary pieces, usually silver with beads and stuff, but I don't think she had the skills to actually manufacture jewellery.'

Arlo held his hand up to the waiter and indicated for him to bring more wine.

'The bracelet wasn't part of the original set. She had that made specially as a gift for me not long before she died. She wanted the set complete.'

Arlo made a mental note not to check for proof of ownership with the bracelet; it would lead him astray.

'Oh, and she gave me a book of drawings of early designs of these pieces, and we've added to it over the years.'

The wine Arlo swallowed got stuck; he coughed and took another large gulp to ease the tickle in his throat that was quickly closing over.

'Are you talking about designs of these black gem pieces?' He tried to keep his voice even.

'Yeah, plus the ones we've created over the last few years together.'

'I'd love to see that book.'

Silvia gave him a quizzical look but their first dish arrived. Gazpacho.

She thanked the waiter and dove straight in. 'It's cold tomato soup!' she declared.

Arlo's mood lifted. This young Australian girl was innocent in many respects. 'Yes, that's what gazpacho is, cold soup. It's perfect for these muggy summer evenings.'

'Okay, weird but I'm happy to try something different.'

Arlo extracted the rudimentary sketches they'd prepared of the yellow diamond earrings. They pored over them as they ate. His eyes darted between the drawing sitting between them and her ears.

She noticed and touched the dangling earrings. 'These are quite different, more of an antique design. This one,' she pointed toward the piece of paper, 'is more elegant, modern, and larger of course.'

'We could replicate some of the fine detail. Why don't you take one off and place it beside the picture?'

Her head shook from side to side. 'Oh, no. We don't want these to be similar. Mine are different, beautiful but distinct. These designs need to be Blanco, specific to your brand and image. Not like these...'

Arlo's jaw clenched. Silvia kept on eating. He lifted his wine glass and downed the remainder before refilling again. Their main courses arrived and Silvia focused on the food. Heat rose from the seafood dish in front of her and she leaned in, inhaled.

'Yum. This smells amazing. Tell me about this dish.'

Arlo's eyes deviated back to the earrings and despite the longing, he let it go. There'd be other opportunities. He turned back into her expectant face and launched into an explanation about the dish of crab, fish and scallops. With each bite, she rolled her eyes in ecstasy.

'I think I've had too much of this fine wine, Arlo.' She offered him her winning smile and his gut twisted. She rested her head in her hand, her eyes drooping.

'Let's get you home.'

Silvia waited at the end of the row of tables while Arlo fixed up the bill. He approached her from behind, pausing momentarily to take her in. She was silhouetted in the silvery moonlight with her face titled upwards star gazing. The pull towards her was magnetic and he moved forwards until he snaked his arms around her waist. Silvia released a deep sigh.

He grasped her hand and twirled her away from the bright lights of the harbour and into a side path.

Before they'd even entered the darkness, Silvia clasped her hands around his neck and kissed him. Her tantalisingly sweet breath brushed his face. It was all the permission he needed.

As their lips slammed together, his pent-up frustration released. The uncertainty about the spinel set, the drain of running the business, of fighting his attraction to her, of being the everything. The kiss was hard and furious, just how he felt. Silvia didn't resist and met him with equal force. She pushed against his body; her breasts leaned onto his chest, her legs in between his. Her arms roamed down his torso, across his waist and bottom.

He lifted the hem of Silvia's summer dress and cupped her bottom, feeling her soft, bare skin. It was cool and smooth. Desire surged through him . . . Silvia unbuttoned the top of his shirt to reveal his chest, her eyes raking over him.

A person walked past and whistled. Common sense and decency came back to him like a slap to the face. He wasn't seventeen anymore, groping girls in alleyways because he had nowhere else to go. And nor was he like his father. This was something he imagined his cheating father would do. Meet women in alleys and kiss them before wandering home to Arlo's mother.

Those thoughts repulsed him. He removed his hands and straightened her dress, smoothed it down at the front and rubbed her arms where goosebumps had appeared.

'Are you okay?'

She nodded. 'Oh, yes. You make me crazy, Arlo Blanco.'

Damn, she made him crazy too. He wanted her and it scared the hell out of him.

Chapter Thirteen

Silvia exited her bedroom wearing her yoga gear. No matter what time her head hit the pillow, or how poorly she slept, mornings meant yoga. She'd done it in her room the last few days, but today she wanted to get out and feel the strong sunshine against her bare skin, the grit of the sand under her feet and allow the sea air to wash over her.

'Hey.' Cruz and Leo sat on the couch and nursed coffees. Most mornings she'd find them here or on the balcony; it was their morning ritual.

'Why are you getting in so late each night?' Cruz asked.

'How would you know anyway, you're not here,' she retaliated.

'Last night was my night off. I was here and you arrived home late, too late to be working. And the night before, Leo said the same. Plus, we haven't seen you at the restaurant for dinner these last few nights.'

Leo flashed an innocent smile of apology.

'What are you? My father?'

'No, only family caring for you.' Silvia was touched but her defences raised nonetheless.

'I'm working. Well, not paid work . . .'

Her cousin cut her off. 'Working at night? C'mon, Silvia . . .'

'No. Wait. It's not like that. I am working. The last few evenings I've been helping Arlo design a new collection. We're doing it together. Last night we had dinner. It's nothing.'

Both men stared at her. 'We were hungry.' She exaggerated the words.

'Arlo Blanco, CEO of *Blanco Fine Jewels*,' he recited what sounded like facts. 'Where did you eat?'

She told them the name of the restaurant and they simultaneously groaned. 'That isn't a quick after-work meal. That is five-star and one of the most exclusive and expensive places to eat on the strip.'

'It was very good,' she said lamely.

Cruz had turned a rather light pallor and rubbed his hands down his face. 'Have you not listened to anything Esmeralda or the family have said?'

'What? What do you mean?'

Cruz looked down and away, resigned. Resigned to what? 'Why does the highly experienced Blanco family require assistance from young women who aren't jewellery designers?'

'Hey.' Annoyance roiled through her. 'I'm actually pretty good. Arlo said so . . .' Voicing the words, Silvia realised how the situation must look. Was Arlo taking advantage of her? Did Carlo Blanco do the same to Paloma all those years ago? Without any breakfast in her tummy, it swished with nausea.

The facts were similar.

Cruz blew out a breath and then spoke with even, steady words. 'It sounds too familiar; a young girl working in the store late at night; there's a change in attitude and sudden loyalty and commitment to the brand, until...there'll be distress and a trip across the other side of the world.'

Silvia stood up taller, and held her yoga mat close to her chest. 'Except I'm here with no plans to run away.' Leo looked away but she kept going. 'You're being ridiculous. Paloma fell in love with Joe and returned to Australia with him.'

The silence of the two men unnerved her. 'I love helping with the jewellery. I think, well, maybe, it's something I'd like to do.'

Cruz moved forward in his seat. 'What? Aren't you returning to continue your medical studies? That's what you've always wanted to do. Like Joe.' He shook his head. 'Strange things happen in that store and lives change.'

'I'm not being forced to do anything, I promise! Honestly, do you think I'd do something I didn't want to?'

'Silvia, he's handsome and rich . . .'

'I don't care about those things.' Some of the force had left her voice.

'Okay. Yes, you're a strong woman. Promise me you'll be careful?'

'I'm fine, honestly you don't need to worry.' Silvia exclaimed with bolstered confidence as she grabbed a banana off the bench and headed out. 'I'll see you later.' She blew her cousin a kiss.

The soft squishy banana flesh was like paste in her mouth and roiled in her stomach. She didn't have a lot of experience with men; had she got this situation wrong? But what was there to misunderstand? Silvia had no misapprehension that the attractive, rich Spaniard was in love with her and they'd live happily ever after. Her heart was secure on that score. But was Arlo taking advantage of her? Using her skills? But she hardly had any, she wasn't a qualified jeweller and was applying her common sense. *Just like Paloma had.*

Yes, she was like Paloma – strong, opinionated and . . . *willing*. Everything was completely consensual though. She'd kissed him because she wanted to. Her drawings were handed over voluntarily. Nothing about this situation spelled coercion or influence. Why then did her chest constrict?

Later that day the door buzzer chimed and a cacophony of noise came through the store. Arlo's heart dropped; he knew those voices: his aunts, nephews and nieces.

He scooted his chair across to the doorway and watched Silvia put away the aerosol cleaning spray and her cloth and stow it under the counter.

'Hello,' they chorused. 'Where's Margo?'

'Hola, I'm Silvia. I've replaced Margo.'

His aunt's face fell, her lips downturned in disappointment she hadn't been told. Arlo squashed the little nugget of guilt.

'Arlo didn't mention he'd found a replacement.'

Silvia wasn't fazed. 'Well, he has, it's me. It's lovely to meet you, I'm Silvia Cooke.'

Arlo's lips upturned slightly at the corners.

'Cooke you say?' his aunt asked in heavily accented English.

His aunt Delores was large and round and wore a flamboyant floral dress with coloured-glass beads at her neck and every finger bejewelled with Blanco.

Elena, his other aunt was short, less stout and demurer. She watched, listened and took in the scene as Delores did the talking. A child hung off each hand while Delores' grandson stormed around the small space screeching like he was driving a race car.

'Yes, Silvia Cooke.'

'You look familiar. I never forget a face.' Delores moved closer to Silvia and scrutinized her features. 'Yes, very familiar. Elena, does she look familiar?'

Elena gazed in Silvia's direction but less fiercely than her sister.

'Can I help you?' Had Silvia's patience run out?

'We'd like to see Arlo please.'

'Who should I say is calling?' Oh, she was good. He was enjoying this.

His aunts were not.

'I'll tell him myself.' Delores lifted the hatch on the bench and walked directly through, the children screamed after her while Elena followed quietly up the rear. Arlo spotted Elena pat Silvia's hand in apology.

Scooting his chair back in place, head bent, he concentrated on the laptop in front of him.

Useless though, Delores yanked him up like a twelve-year-old and crushed him in an embrace. Elena smiled sweetly and rubbed his arm.

'You're not keeping us up to date with changes anymore, huh?'

'Since when have I ever? I didn't realise you were interested in the minutiae of the everyday running of the business, Aunty.'

'You are cheeky boy and no matter what happens, I'll always be your senior.' And without taking a breath. 'Who is that girl? I know that face.'

'That would be difficult given she's Australian.'

That gave her pause before she rattled on. 'It's Arabella's birthday and I said she could choose something from the store, a grown-up pair of earrings.'

Ten-year-old Arabella gazed up at him.

Arlo suffocated his sigh. 'Well, come on then. Let's go and have a look. There's only so many that will suit those dainty earlobes of yours.'

He shouted to the front. 'Silvia, can you please get the trays of small, plain gold earrings that we have? Miss Arabella is turning ten and being gifted her first pair of Blanco jewels.'

'Coming right up.'

Arlo positioned himself in the booth like he would with any customer and Silvia delivered three trays for the girl to drool over.

Delores stood near Silvia and fired off numerous questions asking where she lived in Australia, what she did there and what brought her to their town. Silvia answered with patience and restraint.

Arabella chose a pair that Arlo approved of and she danced on the spot. Delores celebrated the choice and the other children squealed in delight. The earrings were immediately worn but Silvia made a big deal out of handing Arabella the lavender silk pouch. That feeling never got old, even for Arlo. That signature bag brought people a lot of joy, even a ten-year-old.

'We must be off now as we're having a birthday lunch with her parents.' Delores turned back to Silvia. 'I won't be able to stop thinking about you until I remember where I've seen you before. It's going to eat me right up, it is. But I'll remember, don't you worry about that.'

'I won't give it another thought. I promise.' Silvia waved at their departure and gave Arlo an odd look.

Chapter Fourteen

Silvia slammed the apartment door shut upon her return on Saturday morning. She'd gone hardcore on her ashtanga yoga workout, and it had worked. Along with the moisture that had gathered on her skin, her mind had cleared. That's why she was a yoga devotee.

On her return, she'd stopped at *Giuseppe's* and ordered three coffees for her, Cruz and Leo. Plus, a bag of organic fruit. For a young and fit guy, Cruz didn't eat well, except at the restaurant where his food was prepared by a professional chef. Not that it was her job to play mother, but if she bought the fruit, perhaps he would indulge her. At home, Cruz rarely seemed to eat; it was all coffee and cigarettes.

The lads were in their usual spot. She couldn't blame them. That view deserved to be enjoyed.

'Stop!' she said as she entered and Cruz had his cup mid-way to his mouth. 'I've bought you one of the best coffees in town, allegedly. Tell me what you think.' Silvia handed over them over.

Leo asked where it was from and after telling them, she was rewarded with a nod of approval.

'Plus, I've got a platter of fruit.'

'Fruit?' Cruz questioned.

'Yes. Remember what that is? This colourful stuff is good for you. And it's my absolute favourite food.'

'Your favourite food is fruit?' Leo joked. 'You're crazy, sister. So much good cuisine on offer and you choose fruit.'

She bit into a banana as she cut and diced. 'Oh, it's so good. Nothing better than a creamy ripe banana, mixed with a grape or two,' she popped those in her mouth too, 'and sweet and juicy pineapple. Heaven.'

Despite their mocking, they dove on the plate after she'd finished and munched in silence.

'What are you guys doing today?' she asked.

They both shrugged.

'Can you take me to the Pink Poodle?'

Her cousin's words yesterday had played over in her mind. And those *what-if* questions drove her nuts. Guilt had settled in, too. Travelling across the world was about meeting and spending time with the family she'd never known. That she wanted to know. Plus, of course, to scatter her grandmother's ashes. That was scheduled for tomorrow. Since she'd started working at Blanco, she'd spent most of her time with Arlo.

And . . . there was that tiny seed of doubt about him.

Today she wanted to do the right thing and refocus and try to connect with her beloved grandmother once again.

That's exactly what I'm doing in the jewellery store. Yeah, whatever.

'There's not much to see. But yes, we can take you there. It's market day too, so we can wander through and check out the stalls on the way.'

'Oh, man. Can we drive? Those markets are dead boring!' Leo exclaimed.

'Lazy bastard. We must show Silvia the sights, it's not about us. Maybe if there's time later, we can go for a drive up the coast, and show her that Tossa de Mar is not the only divine town. The coastline is pretty special, too.'

Silvia nodded in agreement and continued to munch on an apple. 'Sounds awesome. I'll have a quick shower.'

The market lined the entire esplanade and provided a variety of stalls. Silvia's eyes bulged at the mixture of sweets, lollies and fresh produce along with a variety of sea-inspired trinkets. Shells, bead necklaces, straw hats and photo frames: a collection of all things ocean. A few leather handbags thrown in with beach wear: swimmers, shawls and towels. The boys tolerated her browsing, pausing at some tents and stopping for longer at others. It was the jewellery, whether cheap silver bangles or more unique shell necklaces that caught her attention. Anything with bright colours or unusual designs. Not to purchase, but to consider the intricate setting and combination of gems and beads with stones and made with silver or gold plate. Her creative appetite was insatiable at present and she soaked up each hue, the presentation and dynamic of each item.

It was all stunning, but Silvia was disappointed. It wasn't that different from her local Samford market. In fact, the stuff for sale there was more uniquely crafted with its knitted and crocheted offerings with macramé and beads. Like Tossa seemed to focus on the ocean, Samford took advantage of its country setting.

But still, she'd expected uniquely Spanish jewels, but what did she think that was? The bright pink flamingo earrings? Or Spanish dancers with their full skirts and flamboyant colours? No. But she bought some anyway.

As they neared the end of the row, a fishy aroma penetrated the air and travelled on the breeze. Old timber boats were filled with ice and plenty of fresh fish caught that morning. She spied some prawns and squid, too. 'Should we get some fish for dinner?'

Cruz looked at her as if she spoke Mandarin. 'We'll be having dinner at the restaurant. No need.'

Of course, duh.

Leo led them back into town and the crowds dwindled. Locals sat in small squares and outside their front stoops catching the shade of nearby buildings. It was too early for afternoon aperitifs, so they nursed small espressos.

They advanced along one windy road with black gabled lamps lining the stretch. It led to another square that housed a gigantic church. At the entry were vibrant potted plants surrounded by topiary trees perfectly trimmed into neat circles. The church was the centrepiece, like the gold at the end of the rainbow.

'Wow. This is incredible. Churches at home are not this size. Well, rarely. What's this one?'

Cruz shrugged, clearly unimpressed. To him, they were probably a dime-a-dozen. 'Church of San Vicente. Have a look inside, we'll wait here.'

Leo pulled out a smoke and lit up.

Silvia wasn't religious but the high ceiling was overwhelming and made her feel tiny and insignificant. The interior of the church was cool with its tiled paving and concrete walls. Her thoughts turned to the devoutly religious Paloma. This might have been her parish, where she came each week for service. Had she sat in one of these timber pews and said her prayers?

Paloma had maintained her faith. Silvia didn't pretend to understand but had learned to respect her grandmother's beliefs. Standing inside with the dim lighting and the silence, it felt like her grandmother's embrace. A desperate urge rose within Silvia, to see the Pink Poodle; where her grandmother had lived until she'd left her homeland. A definitive piece of her past. Not a guess.

The significance of this town was not lost on Silvia. This church, these streets and each shop front were filled with connections to Paloma. But her grandmother had given it up. Imagine loving someone so much, you'd give up your life, your family and past.

Silvia walked out of the large double timber doors with their intricate inlay, lost in her own thoughts.

Leo and Cruz rose to meet her.

'Let's go. I'm keen to see the motel.' They commenced walking three abreast and weaving their way around people. They climbed a steep set of worn old stairs. They looked as if they'd been there forever, and perhaps they had. Maybe centuries?

'There's a church in Barcelona, *La Sagrada Familia*, now that's a church. Even larger than that one and it has the most amazing stained glass.' Leo advised.

'I'll have to check it out if I get to the city.'

Cruz was more focused on their task. 'Now, remember, the motel looks different. It's a luxury resort and has been for years. The only thing similar is the sign. You won't miss that.'

'Yeah, okay. I understand. Are there photos of before?'

'I'm sure there are. Maybe my grandparents, but I'd say Esmeralda mostly likely will have them. She's taken a lot more interest in maintaining the past, keeping the memories. Do you want to go and see her afterwards?'

'That'd be great. Thank you,' she reached an arm across his shoulders. 'You're like the brother I never had.'

'Does that make me the cousin?' Leo intervened and shoved himself in between them.

Simultaneously, they shoved him away. 'No!'

Anticipation built in Silvia. Soon she would see the Pink Poodle.

Cruz nudged her shoulder and pointed to the sky as the sign came into view. The tip of a fluffy pink coiffure peaked over the tops of the terracotta buildings. It was lolly pink, bright like an old-fashioned musk. Turning a corner, she squealed. It really was a dog; a poodle dog and the colour contrasted further with a black background and green neon words underneath stating 'motel'. Everything about it was kitsch and seventies and very Miami Vice. And out of place.

The vintage sign didn't fit into its new environs as the resort oozed luxury. High stone walls surrounded the property with tall trees escaping over the top. These were the stereotypical palm trees with a high-rise building up the rear, in the close distance. She stood in the driveway, the only gap in the fence line. It led to a sign-posted reception but gave a clear view of what she'd describe as a concrete monstrosity. Tangerine concrete buildings that didn't match pink, white spray-painted balconies facing inwards, looking down onto paved pathways with compulsory green spaces. An Olympic sized swimming pool, curved into two kidney shapes spread out in front of her. The blue did not compare to the natural topaz of the ocean only metres away. There were slides and a sandy cove with swim-in-bar. The stools were occupied with people drinking from tall glasses with paper umbrellas in various shades of pastel.

'The resort is a bit of a disappointment.'

'Yup. Told you so. Not much of the old motel remains, except the sign. When it was sold, they were hoping to capitalise on its notoriety, but now, it seems old fashioned.'

Silvia captured every angle with her phone. Despite not loving it, she wanted to remember every image. A sad longing swelled up and through her chest, chasing her breath away. She wanted to capture the images to show Paloma, but then realised she would not have wanted to see what it had become.

'Let's go and see Esmeralda. Ask her the questions I can see you are burning to know.'

'Will Savannah or Emilia be there?' Leo asked, his eyebrows rising toward his forehead.

'How would I know?' Cruz said.

'I'll leave you guys to reminisce then, catch ya later.'

Chapter Fifteen

Esmeralda kissed her cheeks in greeting and squeezed them with her thumb and forefingers like Silvia was a toddler.

And like a child, Silvia wanted to wipe away the excess spit and rub the sore spots on her skin.

'Sit, sit' Her Great-aunt gestured wildly. 'I'll get us drinks and snacks.'

Every visit involved food. And not simple finger food taken from the pantry at the last minute. It seemed the Spanish spent their spare time cooking waiting for the unexpected visitors to drop in. No stale potato chips and dip still in its plastic container here.

Esmeralda returned moments later with a laden platter. 'Cruz, prepare Aperol Spritzes; they're perfect for this sultry afternoon, perfect!' she barked as she sat across from Silvia and sank into the comfortable lounge.

'Eat, eat,' she gestured.

Esmeralda spoke most words twice, perhaps for added emphasis.

Besides a few taste tests at the markets, Silvia hadn't eaten for hours so she dove upon that platter much to her aunt's satisfaction.

'I love a girl who eats.'

'I love eating,' she responded.

Cruz returned with a bright orange concoction that she sipped immediately. Large ice cubes clinked against each other as the burst of flavour hit her tongue. She'd seen them selling this drink at the Brisbane International Airport for a whopping fifteen dollars and had scoffed. Now, she drank too quickly.

'That is good,' she exclaimed.

'Is perfect.'

'Aunty, we've been to the Pink Poodle.' Esmeralda looked between them and sat forward in her seat, her legs barely managing to touch the floor. 'Ah, it's rubbish now. Ugly blight on the beautiful horizon of Tossa de Mar. Nothing like when we lived there.'

'Are you saying it was glamorous back in the day?' Cruz chuckled.

'Huh. You joke. It was our home and we didn't know any different. But no, it was not, shall we say, aesthetically pleasing. Except for the poodle. As a kid I adored that pink sign. I still do if I'm honest but my siblings didn't. They were *very* embarrassed. Back then it was so different, so pretty. Well, it was when I was five. When I became a teenager, I confess I may not have brought my friends home.'

'I love it too! It looks like a sign you might find at home on our Gold Coast. But I remember Paloma telling me she hated it.

She shuddered as she described it to me, as if it was distasteful. She couldn't hide her embarrassment even then when spoke about it.'

'Yes, Paloma was older than me and I remember her arguing with our parents about it often. You know what she hated the most?'

Silvia shook her head.

'She loathed sharing the swimming pool. Mum and Dad allowed us to use it whenever we wanted as children, kept us busy of course, but we had to respect the rules and share with the guests. Paloma wanted that pool to herself.'

Esmeralda laughed so that her whole middle shook.

'And she loved swimming. The rest of us would go to the beach when the pool was too crowded through the summer. Not Paloma. She'd keep an eagle eye on it until she spied it empty. And it was always the case that the moment she hopped in, someone would join her. We used to laugh so hard and tease her.' Moisture escaped the old lady's eyes.

'They were good times,' she continued wearing a distant, faraway gaze. Like everywhere in Tossa, there was a view to the water from her home. Esmeralda focused on the view; her mind lost to another time.

'Paloma said the shop was her escape from home, from the motel.'

'Si. She was older then, twenty, was going out on dates, to parties and wanted a more exciting life than the Pink Poodle. She detested helping. The children were expected to pitch in as soon as we were old enough to hold a broom.'

'Do you have photos?'

'Of course!' She waddled across the room and extracted a

thick album. Placed it into Silvia's lap and turned over page after page until she found what she wanted. There were two photographs with the sign on prominent display. Everything about the resort she'd seen today was the opposite to the photo taken back in the 1940s. The motel her grandmother grew up in was only one floor. Like today, the motel building surrounded the pool but with about twenty rooms and not the one hundred or more of the present accommodation. The reception office sat in the same position but wasn't tangerine. Worse, Silvia thought.

'Are the buildings pink?'

Esmeralda turned towards Cruz. 'She asks if the buildings are pink. Of course they're pink!' Her voice rose. 'It was part of the look. The pink dog, pink buildings, the interiors were pink too. Quite turned me off the colour actually.'

Jeez, how could anyone live in a land of lollypops? It must have felt like an amusement park.

'It was successful though; I recall Granny saying that.'

'Uh, huh. Yes, in its day. Our parents set it up on the back of the tourism boom. At the time everyone wanted to holiday at the local beach.'

Silvia kept flicking the pages searching for photos of Paloma.

'But Paloma was smart, she found herself a job. Then she didn't have to clean the guest rooms and wash the sheets. Instead, she came home starry-eyed and life at the Pink Poodle became unbearable for her. Working for Blanco, everything changed. She was never the same. We lost her.'

Her aunt's face was reflective, dream-like for a few seconds before it turned. If Silvia hadn't been looking, she might have missed the fleeting transformation. Esmeralda's lips sneered downwards at their edges while her jaw ground together and her finger pointed.

'It was that old Blanco. He did it. Gave her fancy ideas. That she was better than her family who owned an old embarrassing motel. He changed her.'

Esmeralda sipped her spritz and selected a piece of blue cheese.

'At first, I loved hearing her stories of the expensive gems and shiny gold or sparkling silver. Sometimes I'd lay awake until she arrived home late in the evening. She smelled of alcohol and cigarettes and smiled with happiness. But at some point, she stopped talking as much about the glamorous jewellery and more of the man designing them. His skills, his good looks, him this, him that. I wanted to hear about the expensive gems and the famous people buying them. Eventually she spoke of nothing but him and even I knew as a child, something wasn't right.'

'What did you think was happening?' Silvia asked.

'Ah. It is hard to know what my childhood thoughts were as they are so mixed up now in the adult world. I do know the things she told me, though.'

Silvia leaned forward, resting her head in her hand on her knees. 'What did she say?'

Esmeralda turned it around. 'What did she tell you?'

Silvia looked between Cruz and her aunt.

'She spoke fondly of Blanco and her time at the store. Said she learned so much working there, that it had ignited her love of fine jewellery and she seemed to maintain that passion.'

Her aunt couldn't keep her mouth shut and she interjected. 'Carlo Blanco was twenty years her senior and a married man...' She left the sentence hang for effect.

'She seldom spoke specifically about him.' Silvia paused for a moment, recalling their conversations. She may not remember detail of Carlo Blanco exactly but she did remember Granny's face as she spoke of him: ecstasy, joy, bliss. Silvia did not share this information. 'Why do you hate him and the Blanco family so much?' she addressed Esmeralda. 'Is it because she worked there and not at the motel? Or because it opened a new world for her, exposed her to new things and that took her away from you?'

'Of course, Paloma talked fondly of Carlo. She loved him!' Esmeralda threw up her hands, almost spilling her drink.

'Do you mean in a schoolgirl-crush sort of way? Because she loved Joe. I saw it, I witnessed their love.' Silvia was getting tired of repeating herself. Why did she need to defend her grandmother to her own family? Silvia understood they hardly knew Joe. Would have met him briefly before he whisked her across the world. Did they blame him too?

'She loved Carlo.' Esmeralda's voice was forceful in its conviction. 'It was more than a mere crush.'

Silvia shook her head.

'No, child. You didn't see her wander home dancing on her tiptoes wearing a smile so wide, so happy, that she couldn't sleep for hours. It's true I don't know exactly what happened. I guess no one ever will. But it was only later, when I was older that I learned he was notorious, Silvia, a man who cheated on his wife, regularly. And our Paloma was beautiful and naïve, bless her. We all were back then.'

Silvia looked at Cruz. It appeared as if he didn't know quite what to make of this because he shrugged. 'News to me.'

'She was an adult, I understand. But he was her boss, she was a young sale assistant and inexperienced in the world. He was older and wiser and married and . . . and . . . took advantage of her.'

'Are you sure?' Silvia whispered. Her mind spun with possibilities and her stomach bubbled with nausea.

'Granny was strong. She would have stood up for herself . . .' Silvia's words trailed off.

'Are you spreading gossip, Aunty?' Cruz offered.

'You be quiet.' She addressed Cruz. 'You weren't there. I knew my sister. But as I said. I'm speculating,' she drew out the words. 'But as sure as I am here and breathing, something happened.'

'Did your parents know?'

Esmeralda shook her head. 'No, thank goodness. It would have killed our father. The shame.'

Silvia tried to digest what she was hearing. 'Okay. Even if that is true, she did nothing wrong.' Silvia had to defend her grandmother even though that was silly. 'Perhaps she fell in love with her boss, it happens, and maybe they had an affair. Do you think it ended, whatever it was, when she met Joe...?'

Silvia remembered something else. Paloma had lost a baby. One rainy summer's afternoon, tears had pooled in Granny's eyes as she'd told the story. That child was lost not long after her arrival into Australia. Paloma spoke of the loneliness and despair at the time.

Could that have been Blanco's baby? Silvia shivered. The past as she knew it was changing before her. But of course, Silvia was speculating too. Her poor grandmother having her life dismembered for others to rake through.

Silence like a thick blanket hung in the air. But a steely

reserve came over Silvia. It didn't change her history or the loving relationship she had with her Granny and Pop. That was real.

'There was one night, the only night I saw her distressed,' Esmerelda continued. 'Her hair was wild, her eyes red from crying. That night she lay next to me and didn't speak. Rubbed my back up and down. I was worried about her. But the next morning she woke, her usual self, happy and dressed beautifully for work. The very next day she brought Joe home.'

Silvia was still running scenarios through her mind. Had her grandmother fallen in love with a married man and became a lover scorned? She fondled the necklace she wore. 'Was it the family that gifted Granny this set of jewellery?'

Esmeralda leaned closer. 'I've never seen it dear, but it's distinct Blanco. Old-style Blanco, from the past, but yes, Blanco.' The old lady's lips curled in scorn.

Blanco?

Silvia gripped the necklace tighter and lifted it, trying to get a bird's eye view.

Blanco?

Oh, she was an idiot! It made sense. Did Carlo Blanco gift her grandmother this set before she left? A parting thank you for her hard work?

Silvia bristled. If these stories were true, it was most likely a lover's gift. Something niggled and didn't feel right but she couldn't grasp the thought. Had her grandmother been involved in its design more intimately than Silvia had imagined? Did her grandmother design it? No, she brushed the idea away, she couldn't have. Was she that skilled? In their sessions together she'd certainly been knowledgeable but *that* knowledgeable? But is that why Paloma had the drawings? Is that why she never wore it? Because they brought back too much pain?

Argh! No wonder her family were aghast at her spending time with Arlo. Was she repeating history? Well, to be fair, she was, but not the love affair ending badly bit. Or did it? Carlo was married, maybe they decided any sort of relationship couldn't continue and parted?

Silvia sat back and sighed. Paloma— what happened back then? There were too many questions and not enough answers.

Chapter Sixteen

Arlo gripped the steering wheel, thrust the throttle forward and powered the vessel away from the bay toward the horizon. The wind rattled in his ears and mussed his hair. The loud thump of bass music drowned out becoming a low hum. The clink of glasses and jovial banter, laugher and chat amongst his guests was barely discernible as they got underway.

He loved this boat, *Valencia,* named after his mother. But that was where the sweetness ended. It was all power and he loved being in control of this beast as it sliced through the water at high speed. His luxury cruiser with its leather seats and designer cabin could transport hundreds of people. There was no roughing it over the coastal waters of Spain on Arlo's boat. It was a floating home; everything you needed was at your fingertips.

Today was not a cruise with friends though, it was all VIP, the most valued clientele of the business. Arlo determined to show them the best time in appreciation of their loyalty.

A long, slender, bronzed arm snaked around his middle. Arlo controlled the flinch, but his stomach clenched.

He recognised the cuff on *Miss Spain's* arm. The recent winner in a competition that Blanco sponsored. The pageant was a fabulous supporter of the brand where the top contestants wore their jewellery in a spectacle that was livestreamed to over a million viewers across Europe. The exposure was invaluable. Everyone associated with the competition was their target market and many of them on his boat today.

Miss Spanish wore a tiny, gold string bikini with the thick and solid Blanco cuff on her wrist—one of their best. Ironically, it clashed with her swimmers. It was clear why she'd won; the woman was perfect: flawless complexion and long legs, impressive dark locks tumbling over her shoulders in wavy curls. Arlo kept his eyes fixed on the ocean.

'Can't someone else drive this boat?' she purred.

He forced his mouth into a thin-lipped smile. 'Oh, no, only I can control this high-speed vessel.' The words rolled off his tongue like silk.

She rewarded him with a sexy wink and loaded giggle before gripping the hem of his polo. 'You're wearing too many clothes.' She tugged at his shirt while Arlo moved out of her reach. It didn't work and slender cool fingers slid across his stomach. 'You need to show off that incredible body.' She moved in close, her voice lowered and her voluptuous breasts pressing against him. Slender fingers stalled on his six-pack.

Arlo's concentration did not waver. 'There'll be plenty of time for fun later. I'll be anchoring soon and we can eat lunch and relax, perhaps do a spot of swimming.' Gesturing to the gathered crowd, he continued. 'Why don't you go and enjoy

yourself and have another drink? I'll catch up with you soon.'
He put on his best sultry smile and she kissed him on the cheek
and batted her eyelids before dragging her hands down his torso.
She squeezed his bottom as a departing gesture. Arlo sat down
on the leather seat in the deckhouse and focused on the vast,
blue ocean before him.

His left eye twitched. It must be the glare from the sun, not
because his boat was crammed with some of Spain's most beautiful women. It was a grand sight but what he really wanted was
the guests to open their fat wallets and purchase pieces from the
latest catalogue. Now that would be a successful day.

Irony weighed down upon him. He knew he only had to
click his fingers and he could have any one of these women. All
of this beauty and Arlo only had thoughts of another.

He'd been a fool. He could control himself with these
women who were more striking and charming, but not with
Silvia. She was different; for a start she never threw herself at
him. He admired a girl with self-respect. But she wasn't immune
to his charms and had been a willing participant in their liaisons
so far. Arlo's mind drifted to when he might have the chance to
kiss her creamy, soft skin again . . . he gripped the wheel tighter.

If only he could mould Silvia to his will as easily as these
women. But that would be too easy. The feisty Australian wasn't
one to be trifled with. Why did she have to be so damn attractive? And clever.

Half an hour later, he lowered the anchor into a sandy cove
off a small island where they'd moor for a few hours. Alfonso, an
investment banker slapped him on the back as he stepped down.
Smart guy, he'd always liked him. Perhaps lunch would pass
quickly with some good conversation. Maybe there'd be time for

a swim. He ripped his collared polo shirt up and over his head to soak up the glorious sun.

A waiter refilled his lemon soda and removed his used lunch plate. Arlo was wiping his mouth with a cloth napkin when a commotion kicked up on his right. Glancing starboard, he spotted a tourist boat with large and bright advertising on the side, drifting about five hundred metres away.

What the hell? He jumped up. A woman wearing coloured leggings matched with a white tee and the string of a bikini tied around her neck stood on the deck. Her long dark hair was secured by a baseball cap but he'd know those long legs and stance anywhere. Silvia waved and shouted trying to get their attention.

It was the first boat they'd seen in the hour they'd floated aimlessly on the water. Silvia knew nothing about boating, but even she understood you needed an engine to propel you forward unless you were on a yacht that followed the wind. This wasn't a yacht and something was wrong.

At first the crew had remained as quiet as the silent engines. Called it a break and a chance to admire the view. But the short stop had stretched on. Silvia gripped the railing, placed her feet width apart. It was rocky. When a boat wasn't pushing through the waves it became unanchored and volatile and susceptible to the power and whim of the ocean.

Cruz and Leo had hired the charter boat especially for the occasion. The Garcia family filled both the upper and lower decks. The mood had been jubilant until they'd stalled well short of the vast seas they were heading for.

The family had agreed they'd scatter her grandmother's ashes into the never-ending depths of the deep blue and fragments would float to shore, spreading Paloma along the coast of her beloved Spain.

Excepting that idea was not going to plan.

The Moroccan crew spoke English but chose not to engage when questioned and Silvia grew tired of their belligerence. But she didn't need words. Fear clawed at the pit of her stomach as she watched spanners, pliers and other equipment extracted and held over the engine along with low mumbled conversations and lots of finger pointing adding to the assumption that the engine was kaput.

Why weren't they employing emergency beacons and radios? Perhaps because they thought they could fix it? Silvia held her mobile phone in the air, swivelling on the spot but there was no reception.

They'd been stationary too long when she'd spied the boat and Silvia didn't hesitate.

'*Ayuda!*' She cupped her hands around her open mouth and shouted but she feared the words were swallowed on the wind.

Waving her hands above her head, a man stood and looked her way. They'd heard her! Silvia waved more robustly to keep the boat's attention. Cottoning on to what she was doing, the family gathered around and screamed and grew rowdy too.

The man on the boat moved away, but he pointed and spoke with the others on his deck. Silvia stilled, yes, she was confident they might help.

The luxury vessel was jampacked with people enjoying a good time. She wasn't sure exactly what a superyacht might be, but this one fitted the bill. It was a large boat but even that didn't seem an apt description of the mega cruiser. It had a long-pointed bow that sort of reminded her of those very uncomfortable stiletto heels she had at home. The ones that hurt her feet whenever she wore them because they squished her toes too tight.

On the pointy section of boat, women wearing skimpy bikinis in bold prints, milled about, some sunbaking, others sitting with their legs dangling over the edge. Silvia pulled her cap further down onto her head, tightening it. Hadn't these people heard of skin cancer? They'd burn to a crisp in this bright Spanish sun.

Anyway, it didn't matter who they were. If they assisted, she'd be grateful. She needed to get her family off this dud of a tourist boat. Cruz appeared by her side.

'Hey. This is a disaster. Why did you hire this boat from these losers?' she said.

'Silvia, there's nothing to worry about. They'll tinker around with the engine and get this thing going you'll see,' he said as another loud clunk and expletive floated up from below.

Silvia swatted him on the arm. Cruz swore and looked aghast; at least he had the decency to be embarrassed.

'You are kidding, right?'

'I'm sorry.' He shrugged but stood with his arms crossed. He might run a successful family bistro, but Cruz was just a kid.

The massive cruiser hadn't moved. She was sure they'd seen her. Standing on tiptoes, she craned her neck to get a better look and spotted a speed boat ploughing through the white tips towards them.

Thank goodness. Silvia glanced around checking on her elderly aunts and uncles and the children but no one seemed too concerned to be honest. Sometimes the relaxed European lifestyle did her head in.

The craft slowed as it drew near. She spotted two men, one driving and the other seated. Silvia moved to the stern of her boat where there was a lowered ledge with steps, presumably for people to jump into the water if swimming.

The man driving manoeuvred the speedboat flush to their rear. There was something about the way he held himself that made her do a double take: strong, taut with angular lines. He was bare-chested and as he worked the wheel his back muscles revealed sculpted definition. A turn the other way revealed a chiselled chest with prominent pectoral muscles and six-pack abdominals and a light smattering of hair heading south. As he moved into the sun, his skin glistened with a light sheen of sweat. He turned and faced her and she stared at the aviator sunglasses before her eyes lingered on his bulging biceps when he reached over to pick up a rope.

Silvia caught her breath.

Arlo!

Relief pulsed through her.

Of course, it was Arlo. That man was everywhere. Always when she needed him.

With deft hands, he tied the boat to their vessel, managed himself aboard, and stood in all his bronzed beauty in front of her.

Her stomach was a washing machine of swirling feeling but that could have been the rocky boat. With her focus distracted, she forgot to grip her feet and lost her balance.

Arlo's hand shot out and righted her. His grip was warm and strong. A rush of feeling pulsed through her. Deep down there was relief. She knew this man was secure and reliable, caring and dependable. He was here and she was damn well annoyed at how much that mattered to her.

As he held her tightly, their eyes locked. A fleeting flare of panic flashed briefly in his, then tenderness but too soon, it formed a flashy grin that turned her insides into liquid.

'Carlo?' a voice quavered from behind.

Esmeralda stood on the stoop, her bulk taking up the remainder of the narrow rear platform. Silvia waited for her to realise her error but her aunt stared, her expression glazed.

'Esmeralda.' She placed a hand to her aunt's arm. 'This is Arlo, he's Carlo's grandson.'

Esmeralda lifted out of her stupor liked she'd been woken up from a deep sleep. Her forced laugh held embarrassment. 'Oh, Arlo. You are the spitting image of your grandfather.'

'You knew him?'

Esmeralda recoiled. 'No, my sister did.'

The family gathered around now and crowded in, all speaking at once. The boat dipped with the weight. A crew member came out of the cabin and Arlo spoke rapid fire Spanish. Even with her rudimentary language skills, Silvia knew the exchange wasn't pleasant.

The man presumably disagreed and was joined by a fellow crew member who spoke loudly and gesticulated wildly with his arms.

Even though her family must have understood the exchange, no one intervened. Silvia suspected they realised Arlo didn't need any help and were happy for him to take control.

He turned to her. 'How many in your group?'

'Um, thirty-five?'

'You cannot stay on this tin can. I will have to make a few trips, taking a few at a time.' Arlo started moving, organising her family into groups

'Wait, Arlo. Can you fit all of us on your boat?'

He grinned, a salacious, know-it-all smile. 'My *Valenc*ia? Yes, she can take three times as many. But the little boat cannot.'

He gestured for her to board first.

'No,' she shook her head, 'take my aunts and uncles. And the children.'

Arlo didn't argue. He extracted life jackets from beneath the seats and insisted the children put them on, even the twelve-year old, much to the tween's disgust. It surprised Silvia but pleased her in equal measure. Arlo wasn't the risk-taker she'd imagined, or perhaps not with the lives of others.

She gathered up her belongings and prepared to disembark. There must have been a miscalculation as she was the only one left on board by the last trip. With a free hand she stood close to the edge, ready to catch the tethering rope when Arlo threw it. She'd seen him do it before and it looked easy enough.

With practiced skill, Arlo manoeuvred the little boat into position. Silvia leaned forward ready, but a sudden violent lurch of the tourist boat caused her to overbalance. Bags dropped and her arms flailed, circling to gain traction but she had nowhere to go but forward and she fell headfirst into the ocean.

The frigid water hit her like a brick wall and emptied her lungs of air. She sank and kicked with her legs to return to the surface. Breaching it, she coughed and gulped in air.

'Silvia!' Arlo screamed her name.

Salt water cascaded into her open mouth and she sank once more before arms tightened around her middle, propelling her upwards. She was dragged through the current while splashes pummelled her face. At the boat another pair of outstretched arms secured her and hauled her upwards and over the ridge of the speed boat. Water pooled at her feet as she sucked up shallow breaths of air. Strands of hair hung in her eyes and caught around her ears.

'Are you alright?' Hands scraped across her cheeks and down her chin.

She pulled her head away, used her hands to peel the hair off her eyes so she could see clearly.

Arlo's pupils were dark, his eyes held the recognisable intensity she was used too. Silvia shivered and her body sagged. And because she couldn't help herself, she snarled, 'I can swim.'

He released a laugh and sat back on his haunches. 'Of course, you can. There's nothing you can't do.'

She tried to laugh but coughed instead. A large fluffy towel was placed around her and she clung to its warmth.

The engine started with a roar and with the wind against her moist skin made her body shake. The water was surprisingly cold given how warm the temperature had risen during the day. Maybe a little shock, too, because her leg jiggled and she couldn't stop it. Her teeth chattered and she clenched her jaw to keep it tight.

Men rushed forward to assist when they arrived at Arlo's boat. He had a crew? Of course, he did! Unbelievable. A tall, young man went to help her but Arlo ushered his hands away and he picked her up in one swift movement. He frowned. 'You're freezing.'

Was she? Her body shivered and goosebumps appeared when he'd removed the towel. He hauled her onto the deck; the large vessel was so big, it hardly felt like they were upon the sea. It didn't rock at all.

He carried her to a plush seat on the rear deck and once positioned, overwhelming fatigue swept through her and her eyes drooped. A warm jacket was wrapped around her. Silvia's head lolled to the side and she felt the stiff collar and soft material. As if someone else was operating her limbs like a puppet, she lifted the jacket higher, so it touched her chin. It was Arlo's jacket. First, she smelled salt and seaweed but perhaps that was her skin. When she inhaled again, she smelled him. Cardamon and spice. She snuggled down lower, wanting to wrap herself up in it, in him.

She opened her eyes and wondered if her family were okay. Instead, she spied Arlo near the cabin, wrapped around a woman with striking red hair. Silvia stared at her exposed and smooth-skinned bottom wiggling with delight as she whispered in his ear. The word "womaniser" danced in her head. Trembling, she stood shakily. She was cold and wasn't going to watch Arlo lust after that gorgeous woman. She'd take a hot shower and maybe curl up somewhere warm for the trip to shore.

Chapter Seventeen

Arlo poured himself a neat scotch, drank it in one gulp and placed the glass down before slipping the ring back onto Silvia's long, slender finger.

No need to be frustrated any longer. He knew the truth. Arlo sat on the edge of the couch where Silvia slept. In the end it had been easy. Who knew it would take an accident for him to get the opportunity to examine the jewellery? And of course, to exploit Silvia, all without her knowledge.

The alcohol he'd downed sloshed around in his gut; guilt wracked him. He was human after all.

He was right, though, had known; the ring had the appropriate proof of identity; it was Blanco. What he didn't know was how exactly her grandmother had it in her possession. Given the pieces were declared missing by his family, had Paloma stolen them? It was the only logical conclusion.

His heart twisted at Silvia learning the truth about her loved one.

And was the focus now returning them to their rightful owner? That is, him and the family business? If circumstances were different, he'd have contacted the *policia nacional* the minute he'd discovered the truth. But almost sixty years had passed.

Plus, it was *Silvia*. He gazed at her as she slept, and knew he would never ever, he couldn't do that to her. Besides the scandal would be too great. There was no need to put his family in the headlines unnecessarily. Therefore, he concluded he wouldn't act, but nonetheless, he needed to know more.

And despite what might have happened in the past, Arlo wanted Silvia's creative help finalising the yellow diamond set. '*The Silvia*', the name came to him, yes, he'd name it after her, his inspiration, his muse. It was perfect.

So, the past wasn't his immediate concern, no, finalising *The Silvia*, was his priority.

The rest could wait.

Arlo was contemplating another scotch when Gus jumped onto the lounge and dealt lavish, long tongue strokes to Silvia's cheek.

She roused awake, turning her head from side-to-side to avoid the slobber. Her eyes opened and she leaned on one elbow to push the dog away.

'Gus,' he commanded the dog kneel. A direction Gus ignored and instead, jumped onto Silvia with his heavy weight.

'Gus! Stop it.' Arlo lifted him effortlessly and returned him to the ground where he shooed him away.

'Where am I?' Her voice was croaky from sleep.

'On my boat. Are you feeling okay?'

She didn't answer and sat up, placing her feet square on the ground. Her upper body swayed.

'Whoa. Steady.'

'I'm not a horse.'

'No, but you must be well if you're quick with your retorts. You need a steadying drink.'

Moving through the cabin, he made her something and returned to her side quickly. 'Drink,' he ordered.

And she did.

'Now I feel alive or significantly inebriated. I can't decide which.' Silvia shifted the blanket covering her legs back into position and Arlo rose to get them both another drink. He wasn't the one suffering shock but he needed the strong spirits to still his thrumming heart.

'You remembered,' she said and smiled wider when he produced a banana. He watched each movement as she peeled away the skin.

'Arlo,' she said a moment later, her voice strained, searching around her, under the blankets and through the cushions. 'Where are my grandmother's ashes?'

He stopped her frantic movements with a hand to her arm. 'It's okay. They're here. One of the few things Cruz did do was save them.' Arlo pointed across to the small china urn sitting atop a sideboard.

'Thank you.'

'Next time we'll take my boat out. There'll be no chance of mishaps then. You should have asked me in the first instance.'

'Um, I didn't know you had a cruise-liner,' she rolled her eyes, and paused for a heartbeat. 'You'd do that?'

'Of course. I know how much it means to you.' *Even if your grandmother is a thief.*

Silvia stared at him hard, entering deep down inside his soul and stroking the soft and forgotten parts of him. In a flash, he saw her intensity turn to fortitude. 'Where are your beautiful model friends? The ones who forgot to wear their clothes?'

'Grr,' he imitated a cat growl.

Silvia continued oblivious, 'What was that? A party?'

'No, a business function. I often take important clients out on the boat. It's called marketing. All you have to do is ply people with endless alcohol and they become more inclined to buy my expensive jewellery.'

'Do you sell a lot of jewellery to naked models?'

Her face was dead-pan and laughter erupted out of him. 'Yes, actually and their rich boyfriends and husbands and business owners and bankers and the like. But right now, I assume they're having fun together with Cruz and Leo and your other younger relatives.'

'No!' Silvia searched around the cabin and found it empty.

'Yes.'

'Oh, but what about the rest of my family. They must be worried.' She fussed around again, preparing to get up.

He placed his hand to her leg. 'Don't worry. You freshened up and fell asleep here. None of us wanted to wake you, so they reluctantly agreed to let me look after you. They weren't happy about it, but given I saved your poor asses, they weren't able to mount any valid objections, even though Esmeralda sure did try. She's quite the force, isn't she?'

Silvia released a petite tinkle of a giggle.

'She kept repeating how much like my grandfather I am. I explained I am nothing like either Carlo or my father. She wasn't so sure.'

'Aren't you?'

'We physically resemble each other but that's where the similarities end. They both have certain qualities I do not emulate.'

'Interesting . . .'

'Yes, Esmeralda thought so too. She very much dislikes my grandfather.'

'Yes. The family blames him for Paloma leaving and never coming back. They say she changed after she met Carlos; while she worked in your store. Rightfully or not, they blame him for the pain they experienced at her loss. But I'm sensing it's easy to lay blame at someone else's door and not examine one's own behaviour.'

'What do you mean?' A frisson of something passed through him.

'They believe a certain version of what happened, but I've heard my grandmother talk, she glowed, Arlo, reminiscing about her time in Tossa de Mar. The jewels, your business, her time working in the store with Carlo. Those were fond memories.'

'What does your family say?'

'They have a much darker view; they say she fled Tossa. That, that, perhaps . . .'

'What?'

'Something was going on between her and Carlos. I'm sorry, I know he was married.'

Arlo's body went stiff, his shoulders locked in place. 'Just so I'm clear, are your family saying that Carlo had an affair with

Paloma and they concluded this affair and she fled to Australia?' His words were like ice.

Silvia nodded. 'Basically. They are very confident, vehement in their suggestion. But I saw my grandmother with her husband Joe, she loved him. She moved to Australia with Joe when he was returning home because she loved him.' She paused. 'But despite that, I think...maybe parts of what they say might be true.' She twirled the ring around her knuckle.

Yes, what happened before Paloma left? The words were unspoken and he dare not ask them. Dare not seek the truth. He wasn't ready.

'What was he like? Your grandfather?' she asked.

This he could answer easily. 'He was ruthless and scrupulous in both his business and personal life. One hundred percent committed to the jewellery. He was a harsh father and a terrible critic. Unfortunately, my father has those same traits.'

Sympathy passed across her features before being quickly replaced with a grin. 'You all sound similar to me.'

'We are nothing alike.' He jumped up, needing that drink. He didn't want Silvia to read his expression, the hard set to his lips and clench of his jaw.

He kept his back to her and poured a shot and drank it straight down. 'Why don't you speak to your family, assure them that you're well.' He paused, turned, 'Will you have dinner with me? We can head back to my place and maybe order some dinner? Perhaps we can finish our designs and next week we can send them to the production team?'

'You're going to have them made into real pieces?'

'Yes. I think they're extraordinary.'

'I do too. And yes, I'd love to have dinner with you. I'll ring my aunty and we'll get going.'

He nodded and turned away.

They worked in his home office until the sun sank over the horizon and was gobbled up by the sea.

'What do you think?' Silvia held up a further sketch of the necklace. 'I've made a subtle change here, where the chain joins the gem. Do you like it?'

He took it into his hand and considered it, taking his time. 'I think you have a real knack for designing jewellery. It's your attention to the fine detail that sets unique and special jewellery apart from the rest. From the ones you buy at the chain store in the city, that are mass produced on a production line. The detail you've added here,' he pointed to the crux of it, 'adds so much to the necklace. It focuses our attention to this large square yellow diamond. Exactly as you said it should right from the start.'

'Wow. Thanks, that's quite a compliment.'

They hadn't mocked up the bracelet but smaller versions of the earrings, necklace and ring were laid out before them.

'I cannot wait to see them produced. Do you think we're done?'

He nodded. 'Yes. Sometimes the team provide further ideas in the actual making of the piece. Sometimes a setting doesn't work as we've drawn it, and usually they are spot on. HQ is in Barcelona and I must attend a jewellery fair there soon. You can come with me?' Then he softened his tone. 'If you'd like.'

'Oh wow. Barcelona. That would be fabulous. Is that okay? Am I allowed to come?'

He sat back and hadn't realised his own heightened sense at her anticipated response, but when she said yes, the knot of tension in his gut unravelled. 'Of course, you are. I'm the boss.'

'Oh, yes, I remember. It's not easy to forget.' She tilted her head, offering a coy smile through batted lashes. 'I'm starving. We didn't actually get any lunch on that boat today and I've had nothing but your banana.'

'Don't worry about that ridiculous tourist trap, I'll have them sorted out. The money they charge innocent tourists and don't have their equipment up to scratch.' His tone was business-like. 'What do you feel like eating? More traditional Spanish paella or something different? There is a fabulous Chinese take-out I use all the time and they deliver.'

'Aww, you aren't going to cook for me?' She pouted.

'I can cook but I'd rather spend the time with you.' The air around them charged and turned electric.

No hesitation from Silvia. 'Let's have Chinese then.'

After he'd ordered, he delivered her a glass of chilled Chablis.

'Can you give me a tour?'

'Of course, I'd love to. We have at least half an hour before the food arrives.'

He showed her the best first, of course.

'I mean, wow, Arlo. This is spectacular. Please tell me you don't take this view for granted?'

He stood close to her on the balcony that curved around the rear of the house and faced the ocean and cliffs below. The town of Tossa de Mar glimmered to their right with its bright street-lights and occasional neon signs along the tourist strip. Below, in dark contrast to the sea that roiled and rallied against the cliffs, sat an electric blue pool illuminated and shimmering.

'What's that?' she asked and pointed below.

'That is another balcony that hovers above the cliff face. I initially had the base made of glass so that you could look at the cliffs below and be mesmerised but most people are too scared to walk on it, so I made it a covered walkway with glass barriers. It's a fantastic spot to watch the sun set. And to answer your question. I don't take this for granted. This wasn't given to me by my family. I earned this house. I paid for it through hard work. I strive to make the business the best it can be.'

'Okay, I understand. I get it.'

'This place is my haven. My retreat. When the world gets a little too hard, I come home and it helps me find perspective.'

'Does the world trouble you often?'

'Not usually, but more so lately.'

He could tell she wanted to ask more but he wouldn't talk about that. Arlo just wanted to be with her. He held up his flat palm. 'Let's finish the tour.'

Midway through the tour, the doorbell chimed and the smell of black bean beef stir-fry permeated the air and lead them back to the main living area, the heart of the house. Lucky, they'd been about to enter his bedroom. Would she be embarrassed in his private space? Somehow, he didn't imagine Silvia would flush red as seeing his masculine abode with its deep browns and dark hues.

'Who would have thought the Spanish could do Chinese so well?' she said as she shovelled in another mouthful of fried rice.

'It's run by Chinese.'

After they'd finished their meal, Silvia took off her ring to wash the few dirty dishes. It slipped easily over her knuckle and he watched her gaze sweep between it and where she placed it on the bench, and him.

'You don't have to do that. I have paid help.'

She rolled her eyes. 'I'm capable of cleaning up.' Arlo picked up the ring and worried it between his thumb and forefinger. He put it back down. Silvia chewed her lower lip before sinking her hands into the suds of the sink.

'Nightcap?'

'Mmm, yes please.' She finished the dishes and wiped her hands on a tea towel when he handed her a crystal glass. 'What's this?'

'Vermouth, it's complex and full of spice. So much better than brandy.'

'If you say so, bottoms up,' she said as she sipped.

'I thought you were Australian, not English.' He smirked and drank the liquid in one mouthful.

The heat of the alcohol warmed his chest. With sudden clarity, he realised he wanted the evening to linger; wanted her to stay, talk with him and he'd admit, he was desperate to kiss her again. Now as he watched her, he remembered the curve of her bottom under his hand. The pressure of her legs entwined with his. The cup slipped from his grip and rattled against the bench; he covered the gesture by refilling it with too much liquid.

An unwanted image of his mother entered his mind. Late, darkness prevailing outside, the humidity still clinging to their skin like blankets, the two of them sitting side-by-side on the lounge in their home, silent tears rolling down Valencia's cheeks before she wiped them away. Her face filled with anguish after yet another night of his father slinking home smelling of cigarettes and alcohol, and worse, another woman's perfume.

He placed his flat palm on the bench and blew out a breath. He wasn't his father; he wasn't an adulterer and could control himself and his own behaviour. If he had Silvia, he wouldn't stray. But she might? His ex-wife had. Just like his father.

That didn't stop the testosterone surging through his body, making him want to take her now, to push her against the kitchen wall and feel her curves and supple breasts and her heart hammering against his chest. His blood ran thick and fast through his veins.

'Is that a spa?' she pointed to the far reaches of his lower-level balcony. It sat perpendicular to the pool and house.

'Yes.'

'Can we use it? I've still wearing my bikini.'

Oh, yes, he wanted to scream. The outline under her shirt had driven him wild all day.

'Sure.'

It wasn't in Silvia's nature to flirt. That was for other girls, the popular ones, more beautiful and confident than her. But there was something about the way Arlo looked at her, that made her entire body tingle with want; the way his desire pooled off him and his eyes always focused on her lips and his mouth would open, like he wanted to gobble her up. It gave her confidence and a sense of, dare she say it, sass.

A low level of heat simmered between them. It was incredibly erotic to be so aware of someone else and their every movement: an intake of breath, the rise and fall of his chest, a bob of his Adam's apple as he swallowed. His fragrance alone was driving her crazy. She wasn't sure she could take much more but then the doorbell had chimed and she'd blown out the breath she'd been holding. His hand had been on the doorknob and they were about to enter his bedroom. She'd been certain if he was going to kiss her again, the bedroom would be the perfect spot: dim and dark and inviting. But damn, the food had arrived.

All afternoon she'd sensed a hesitation in him that didn't fit with his brusque manner and playboy image. Was it possible there was a softness to Arlo Blanco or was he holding something back?

And right now, frankly she didn't care. She wanted him, bad.

At the spa, she faced the expansive ocean and pulled her tee over her head. Placed it on a chair before reaching for her leggings and tugging them down around her ankles. Without looking at him, she stepped into the warm water of the spa. The surface remained still, no life in it yet. Lowering her body until her legs were covered, she spun around and sat on the ledge.

Oh man. She wished she'd turned sooner.

Arlo was frozen, his arms hanging by his sides. His tongue flicked across his lips and his chest rose and fell. He stood wearing only his swimming trunks. His bare torso on display. It was smooth and clear and she wanted her hands on that skin.

She sank lower, her body covered by the water as Arlo took slow deliberate steps towards the spa as if trying to keep a measure of control.

There'd been an innocent sense that she hadn't been sure

what was going to happen when she'd asked to hop in the spa. Now, she was certain. The intense look in his eyes drank her up once more and she knew that if he'd been restraining himself, that he was not going to any longer.

He was barely in the water when the bubbles began and the water swirled around them. It created white noise and drowned out her own thoughts. She reached for him immediately and he did not hesitate.

Their lips smashed together with haste, desperation, longing. Their bodies crushed against one another, nothing left to hide; nothing left unexposed, everything on offer. Arms entangled, legs swooped around middles and hands teased every bare spot. Frenzied and fast. He tugged at her bikini string and flung it to the side. His hands were gentle on her breasts, unlike their kisses. His thumbs circled her nipples and they responded by standing to attention. He lifted her onto the upper step to allow him more room. His mouth found one breast then the other. His hands cupped her soft flesh.

Silvia clasped his bottom and pulled him closer until their groins were perilously close. Their mouths reconnected; their tongues clashed. The turbulent water swirled over them, their bodies slick and smooth to the touch. He kept her on the step and rose to remove his swimmers. Silvia gulped and once he was submerged, she pushed her hands through the water until she found him. Moving to take off her bikini bottoms, he stilled her hands.

Instead, he pulled one string down her thigh, followed by the other. He pulled her upwards to standing and traced that string down her bare legs until she stood naked before him. He rose, their bodies met, their hearts hammering in rhythm and breaths flowing fast. There was the crinkle of a wrapper and the movement of him rolling on the condom. Done, he grasped the nape of her neck, kissed her again, deep and frustrated and urgent before leaning her gently against the rim of the spa. He nursed her back and dragged her down with him, their bodies together, into the water. The water splashed over the edges as their bodies moved together.

She clutched his back, clawed at his skin before she forgot about everything else.

Chapter Eighteen

One week later they were on their way to Barcelona. Arlo drove fast along the coastal route showing off the picturesque Costa Brava region. It would be a short trip in his silver Aston Martin that hugged the curves in the road.

Silvia had admired the car when he'd raced to a stop to collect her. Climbing in, her body sank into the deep, leather bucket seat. 'It feels like I'm in a James Bond movie and we are running from the baddies who are shooting at us around each corner.'

'Does that make me James Bond?' he joked.

'I guess it does.' She admired his look. Arlo wore well-fitted pants with a blue collared business shirt minus a tie and matched with canvas shoes rather than his usual Italian leather boots.

'You fit perfectly with the car which is incredible.' She traced her fingers along the timber trim on the window. 'We could be on an amusement park ride, strapped in, ready to go too fast and roll through the bumps.'

'That's where you're wrong, there'll be no bumps. This baby is smooth.'

'Kind of like it's owner!'

One hand to the wheel, the other gripping the gear stick, Arlo leaned over to kiss her. His eyes sought permission and without hesitation, Silvia met him halfway.

He didn't need to ask to kiss her after what they'd shared over the last week. They'd done way more than kissing. But Arlo desired to make her happy, to see that smile glow upon her face, her eyes light up with delight. She was so easy to please, so happy with any gesture that he made.

What made him uncomfortable was his need to always be near her, feel her silky-smooth skin and the smell of her sweet breath. She was intoxicating and Arlo felt like he was perpetually drunk.

'These are for you.' He reached into the back of the vehicle and handed her a bunch of red carnations with one sole bright yellow bud amongst them.

'It's huge!' She exclaimed and immediately buried her nose into the bunch to inhale their scent.

'Red carnations are our national flower. Aren't they spectacular?' Arlo didn't admit that he'd bought out the local florist's entire supply. And had paid handsomely for the privilege.

'Yes, they are. We have a few carnation bushes growing at home in our garden. Not this colour though, only pale pinks and some white. These are something else.' Silvia inhaled again before placing them in her lap and leaning over for another kiss. 'Thank you, they're gorgeous.'

Arlo warmed at her praise.

'I bought a bunch for my mother, too and dropped them off on my way here.'

'That's sweet. Do you often buy her flowers?'

'Not as often as I should. She deserves them.'

It was a straight drive of less than ninety minutes, plus, familiar with the road he hardly had to pay attention. Occasionally, Silvia called out something of interest and he'd notice it for the first time.

'Tell me about Samford,' he said.

So, she did.

'You love it there.'

'I do. It was home because that was where my family was. Now there's no one there.' Her face clouded over.

'That's true, but it can always be special to you. All those memories.'

She agreed.

'Tell me about medicine and what you love about it?'

'Medicine?'

'You sound surprised, but you have completed half a medical degree and are enrolled to finish it, right?'

She laughed with no sincerity. 'Yes, of course. But it feels like a different life. Being a doctor is what I've always wanted to do. My grandfather was an excellent doctor, caring, compassionate and such a people person. You know how some doctors don't listen properly or rush through your consult? He was never like that and often came home, quite anguished about the current condition of one of his patients. He was wonderful under pressure.'

'He sounds like a great man.'

'He was special. Regardless of any silly questions or

wondering about this or that as children do, he always had time for me.'

'You would be the same kind of doctor. However, your prescriptions might be yoga and fruit!'

She slapped him on the leg. He caught her hand and captured it on his thigh. The mere touch sent a warm shiver hurtling down his leg.

They settled back in silence for a while until he turned at a soft snuffle; Silvia had fallen asleep. He placed her hand back on her lap and concentrated on the road.

Hard to do, as he inhaled her intoxicating womanly scent. He swore he'd never tire of that smell; it was simple and under-stated, innocent, yet strong and alluring. All woman. There was nothing light and floral about Silvia; she was bold with fresh undertones. It wasn't only her aroma, she stimulated him in ways he hadn't experienced before. Conversations were never dull, they discussed topics he hadn't thought of before that kept him captivated. He could listen to her talk for hours and forget to utter a word. She wasn't like Spanish women, often loud and brusque, dominating; the Australian in her demonstrated a fun-loving nature that only turned serious occasionally.

Anticipation built within him. He wasn't usually prone to emotion but he was excited to show her the sights of his favourite city, Barcelona. Cosmopolitan and vibrant, it was a great place to visit. He wanted to experience it with her: the food, galleries, architecture, but most of all, the jewellery fair. It was the largest jewellery fair of its kind and held annually in loca-tions around the world, and this year, his city. A massive coup for the country and an important event for *Blanco Fine Jewels*. He'd been to many important jewellery conventions, but this one would be special; this one would reveal the greatest new design he thought his company and perhaps European jewellery houses had seen for years. His foot planted on the accelerator, keen to cover the distance.

But moreover, Arlo couldn't wait to share the finished jewellery with Silvia and reveal he'd named it after her. He glanced across at her sleeping form. She'd be returning to Australia soon. Maybe they could work on something else together before she left? Yes, that was a damn fine idea. The pedal lowered again and he caught himself driving too fast.

This beautiful woman from Down Under was under his skin. It was easy to forget that her grandmother was a potential thief. Even easier to forget he'd kept Silvia close for the purpose of uncovering information about the black gem, facts now in his possession. Plus, she'd provided the creative inspiration he so desperately needed. Silvia Cooke had been useful to him. The betrayal to the family business seemed less important now. But none of that explained why his gut twisted at the prospect of her leaving. When he looked at her, a pain developed in his chest. Was it because Silvia would take her talent and leave and he'd have no more ideas without her? It wasn't because her eyes shone when she smiled, or that her petite body fitted neatly under his arm, or that her kisses swept him away to another place, was it?

Arlo sensed he could trust her, problem was, he wasn't sure he could trust himself.

Compared to the small coastal town of Tossa, Barcelona was big and chaotic. The place was crazier than Brisbane at peak hour! Entering the outskirts of the metropolis, Silvia had roused awake to the sounds of beeping horns, revving cars and the violent dinging of bicycle bells. She'd opened her eyes to see a blue sky murky with traffic exhaust and locals and tourists streaming along the sidewalks of the city streets. Her chest lurched with a sudden longing for her patch of grass at Samford. It was the opposite to this: peaceful, quiet and slow-paced.

Arlo parked in a street lined with shops and restaurants and high-rise apartment buildings. 'We'll drop off our stuff and have a quick bite to eat. I've brought provisions and then we'll head out to explore. There is so much I want to show you.'

He exited the car and rushed around to her passenger door and held it open for her to alight. They were outside a three-story apartment building with a café downstairs and a strip of shops either side. After extracting their bags from the boot, he let them in with a key.

'My brother isn't home until tomorrow, so we've got the place to ourselves.'

'He's not here?' Silvia repeated.

'Yes.' Silvia waited for more information but Arlo wasn't forthcoming.

The apartment on the top floor was spacious and modern over three levels. Black and white photographs of women, children, landscapes and even some Blanco jewellery covered the walls.

'Come and have a look at this.' Arlo gestured her toward the outdoor balcony. He slid open the glass door which let in a cacophony of day-time noise. Silvia moved to the edge and peered over.

'Oh my gosh. What is that?'

'That is *La Sagrada Familia*,' and he waved his arms in an arc to take in the impressive structure.

'Gaudi,' she whispered.

'Yes, the Roman Catholic Basilica designed by Antoni Gaudi. We'll visit after we've eaten. It's impressive.'

Silvia stared at the church and felt a bit starstruck but Arlo's embrace from behind provided distraction. She clutched his hands to her middle and held them there and closed her eyes to retain this image and feeling, forever.

They ventured back inside and he offered her a glass of wine.

'With lunch?' she laughed.

'Of course, it is the Mediterranean way,' he said and his hand hovered, their fingers linking over the stem of the crystal. She didn't take the glass and he retrieved it and placed it down on the table and pulled her toward him, their hips meeting in perfect union. Arlo placed a solitary finger to her lips tracing their outline before laying a trail of kisses along her chin until he met her neck where he nuzzled until she groaned.

'That tickles.'

One hand held the nape of her neck as their mouths met. The relief was instant.

'I've been wanting you to do that all day.' She met his kiss with equal pressure, equal need.

'Lunch can wait,' he said, his eyes glassy and hooded. She nodded and cast another glance at the church. He followed her gaze.

'There's another place that Gaudi designed called *Park*

Guell. It's a parkland filled with similar designs and more colour. I'll take you there as well. Soon, after.' He trailed fingers along her arm until he held her fingertips tightly and stepped down the hallway, ensuring she was following.

'Can you take me everywhere?' she asked, her voice low and sultry as she reached for him.

Chapter Nineteen

The next morning Arlo drove underneath a building of modern, architectural design.

'Is *Blanco Fine Jewels* always represented at these conventions?'

'Yes. Each major jewellery house of Europe will be present.'

'It's a strange concept. A convention to show off to your competitors when the objective is to make sales. Other creators aren't going to buy your products, surely?'

Arlo flinched at the word *products*. 'Our jewellery is not merchandise. That refers to mass-produced items.'

'Okay, I'm sorry, wrong word. But you know what I mean.'

He reverse-parked the Aston and waited for her to alight before he clicked the car shut.

They walked together to the lift. 'The objective of these trade fairs is for companies to show their latest ideas, meet with industry experts and customers, study activities of rivals and examine recent market trends and opportunities. Press attend, too. There's lots of showing-off but that's part of the fun. I'm told when I attend, the numbers double.' He offered her a sly, cheeky smile.

'I'm sure.' She leaned over and gave him a lingering full-lipped kiss before the lift doors opened to reveal throngs of people walking around an impressive array of stalls. He glanced across at her and smiled.

'Oh! There's a lot of money in this room.'

'Yes,' he agreed. To Silvia he was sure the displays would seem elaborate and overdone. What would she think of Blanco? He'd find out very soon as they paused in front of the familiar red sign.

It was a grand, ostentatious and striking stand. Staff rushed forward to greet him and offer congratulations on the newest collection.

He hung back and watched Silvia swerve around the gathered group and enter the site. She was immediately drawn to the glass display in the front of the stall with its yellow and white diamonds sparkling with exquisite unblemished and pure gold. Arlo had been dumbstruck when he'd first seen it, too.

The noise around him receded as he watched Silvia.

He approached her from behind. 'What do you think?'

'Is this, is this, our collection? The pieces we designed?'

'Yes.'

Her eyes flicked to the rear of the case and the sign that read *'The Silvia Collection'* and back to the jewels in the centre. Her eyes widened, her lips parted and a hand flew to her chest. She was speechless and this was the best reaction, exactly how it should be, the admirer unable to speak of its beauty.

Arlo gestured for the security guards surrounding the exhibition to move aside. He extracted a key and opened the case to remove the necklace before placing it around Silvia's neck with slow and measured movements. He removed the simple earrings she wore and replaced them with the gems from the display. He dressed her until she wore the entire set worth hundreds of thousands of dollars.

She glanced downwards and lifted her finger to examine the ring and bracelet; touched her ears until there was a frantic flash of lights. Cameras were in her face and Arlo was pushed back. She blinked like a deer caught in headlights and instinctively raised her hands to cover her face.

'Move back everyone,' Arlo said, not wanting to discourage the attention but to call order to the commotion. 'Let me through and we'll move our model into better light and you can capture the shots you want.'

He steered Silvia by the elbow toward the rear and in front of a makeshift backdrop of an exotic Mediterranean scene. Once in place, he stood with his back to the crowd. 'What do you think?' he whispered. Her fingers explored the gems around her neck and her eyes darted around her as if trying to make sense of the scene.

Finally, the words he longed to hear. 'They are beautiful.'

Arlo nodded, satisfied and turned back to the melee. 'She's all yours, gentlemen.' He moved to the side and let them go crazy with their cameras to capture the perfect shot. Arlo hadn't thought about what he might say to the media, but the words rolled off his tongue. Months of collaboration, fresh, new ideas, precision design, yellow diamond centrepiece of the most valuable quality and without a doubt, their next best thing.

As each piece of jewellery was removed, Silvia's body lightened. The pieces, particularly, the necklace, were heavy. Much heavier than she would have imagined. They were everything she'd dreamed: bold, bright and beautiful. And Blanco. All Blanco.

Arlo engaged with the media and spoke with people Silvia imagined were buyers, designers and retail outlets. The minutes dragged on as he wooed his audience.

Tired of watching, and keen to be out of prying gazes, she moved away and dawdled amongst the other sites. Her eyes boggled at the vast number of jewellery houses in Europe and their incredible accessories. Gazing at each of them in turn, a strange fizzy sensation settled in her stomach. So much beauty, so much creative expression and so much money in one place. Plus, the possibilities! Her stay in Tossa de Mar had ignited a fierce passion for jewels, not that she belonged here amongst these greats, but ignoring that she felt like a fake, she fished around in her bag for a notebook and scribbled down the ideas swirling around her head.

'I hope you aren't plagiarising our inventions in that secret little pad.' A man stood close, his arm brushing hers.

'Oh, no. I'm sorry. I wasn't, I promise,' she stammered.

'No, me, I'm sorry. Please forgive me,' he said no doubt responding to her stricken face.

Silvia's heart slowed down and she lowered her hand from clutching her chest. The man was model good-looking, perfect in every way. Asymmetrical dark and stormy eyes in a finely chis-elled-face, smooth skin that was covered in a short, neatly trimmed beard and hair that sat in perfect curls.

'Are you familiar with *Maison de Bijoux*?'

She shook her head and he acted wounded, holding his hand to his heart.

'Ah, well now you are.'

'French?' That explained the accent.

'Ah, *oui mademoiselle*. House of Jewellery. The best jewellers in France. Come see.'

Silvia followed him into the store and knew immediately it wasn't her style. It was garish brooches and large pendant-type necklaces. Jewellery she imagined an elderly grandmother—not hers–would pass onto their granddaughters. The sort royalty might wear. There were peacocks with a bright variety of colours across the wings, an eagle with an oversized diamond eye and Picasso typestyles with strong lines and odd shapes.

'It's unique.'

'Yes!' He mistook it for a compliment.

'Who's your clientele?' She was fascinated with who would purchase and wear such pieces.

'The rich and famous of France. The First Lady is one of our best supporters.'

He placed his hand to the small of her back and directed her towards their display. Blanco prided itself on the finest quality of stones exuding what she thought was elegance, expertise and undeniable beauty. Particularly *her* design. Here, heavy, chunky and over-detailed pieces hung from the arms of a makeshift Moulin Rouge windmill. The colours clashed and the scene assaulted her eyes so she had to look away.

The pressure on her back was warm through her thin cotton blouse. The man kept it there and held her close.

'I am Julian. Where are you from? England?'

'No, I'm Australian.'

'Ah,' he continued. 'Land of deadly animals and hot sun.'

'Um, yes, I guess that sums it up.'

'You are designer?' he nodded towards her notepad.

She shook her head and put the pad away. 'No. I enjoy crafting beautiful jewellery but I am not a professional.'

'Ah, what's a professional anyway? What you think? If you could design a brooch representing your country, what would it look like?'

Nothing like these ugly specimens.

She wracked her brain; a brooch was so old-fashioned she'd never considered creating one before. 'Um. There could be so many elements. A koala or kangaroo would be common so would any of our many landmarks. They would only make cheap souvenirs. I might choose a wattle leaf.'

'A what?' he asked.

Silvia fished out her mobile phone and searched for a picture.

Silvia was getting into the idea now. It would be dark metal something like tarnished brass with delicate diamonds along the front edge and the wattle flowers made of yellow crystal. Not diamonds this time.

'We could design it together, this wattle.'

Silvia wasn't sure she heard him correctly. 'And if we did, would I get any credit?'

He smiled, 'Of course. You and me together. The Australian and the Frenchman.'

'And if we were here showing the finished product,' she deliberately chose that word, 'would you acknowledge my contribution?'

His eyebrows raised towards his forehead but he nodded.

'And would that lead to profit-sharing?'

Julian's chuckle was low and uncomfortable and when he spoke, his accent was accentuated. 'Our designers work for the company and are given full credit but not profits.'

'Oh, I'm sorry I was just wondering how these things worked.'

And it was very interesting indeed.

'Jules.'

That deep and honey-toned voice made her body thrum. Arlo arrived next to her and with authority but no fuss, moved her into a position where Jules could no longer touch her.

Jules appeared pleased to see him and kissed Arlo on both cheeks, followed by a too-heavy slap to the back.

'How's business, man?' Jules asked but before allowing Arlo to answer, he looked at Silvia. 'I should have known you'd know this beauty. You get all the gorgeous women.'

'I don't think you have any trouble in that regard,' Arlo joked and kept his tone civil but Silvia could tell he didn't like Jules. It was the throbbing vein in his neck that gave him away.

'What about the convention? Going well for you?'

'Of course,' Jules replied and talked of his successful sales and prominent persons to have browsed their stall. The name dropping brushed off Arlo.

'Nice to see you. We're off.' He held his hand out to Silvia who ignored it. 'Nice to meet you,' she said as Arlo called her away.

'Julian?' She turned back. 'Have you seen the newest Blanco piece?'

'Ah, yes of course. Who hasn't? It is *tres jolie*. Very Blanco.' He waved her on.

'You know him well?' she said to Arlo as they walked away.

'Yes. It's a family business, too. They've been around for as long as I can remember. His father and grandfather ran it before him too. We have that much in common.'

'But not much else?'

'You are very perceptive.'

Chapter Twenty

'You haven't said much about the collection. Are you pleased to finally see the finished pieces?'

Silvia stared straight ahead out of the front window of the car. Then she turned in the seat and faced him as he battled the Saturday night traffic. 'When were they made?'

'Over the last week.'

'And you saw the collection before today?'

'Yes, of course. I oversaw every step. I've travelled up to Barcelona several times.'

Silvia extracted a banana from her bag, peeled the skin down on each side and then bit off the top. 'We spent hours debating the tiniest of details over each piece, particularly the necklace, night after night labouring to make it perfect, and the last time we talked about it, you told me that you'd have your team make them.'

'Y-e-s,' Arlo drew out the single word.

'Perhaps I misunderstood but I thought they were simply

being mocked up and then they'd return to us for finalisation and approval.'

He opened his mouth to confirm that's exactly what he'd done but she kept speaking.

'Then with incredible speed *your team,*' she emphasised the words, 'creates pieces you were ready to introduce to the world at your jewellery convention and receive the accolades for designing the next and newest wonderful Blanco creation.'

Arlo had a sinking feeling this wasn't going well. 'I named it after you. The name suits the set; it's a testament to you and your idea.'

'Did you consider that I might have liked to see the individual jewels before the rest of the world?'

'I wanted to surprise you.'

'Oh, you surprised me all right. What a privilege to model the jewellery for the first time in front of the world press with no acknowledgement that I had co-designed them with you.'

'Silvia...'

'I came up with the original design, you remember that, right? That small detail has been forgotten and now I've been relegated to being the model?'

The words hung in the stale air of the car.

'Silvia, that was never my intention. It . . . I . . .' The words faded away until he continued, with more umph and fight. 'You knew you were helping me design a set for the company. I was always honest about that and the fact that I needed a grand new idea to wow the market and keep the company performing well.'

'Yes, you were and I never expected to take a cut or in any way profit from the idea. But I also never expected to be blindsided in public with no acknowledgement of my contribution.

You could have given me that privilege alone and then shown it off however you wished. But you didn't. You know...' The tone of her voice rose, became shrill.

'I'm wondering if Carlo did something similar to Paloma. It appears she had skill, perhaps the same talent you claim I have. I think she helped design the black spinel and then something . . . something happened, I don't know what. But after what's happened today, I wouldn't be surprised if she helped like me and received no credit and then Carlo wanted to do something with them that she disapproved of —'

'Those spinel pieces were always Blanco. The pieces we worked on together were always Blanco.' His voice was cool and exacting.

'You knew...?' The silence in the car was deafening. Arlo couldn't look at her. He kept his eyes peeled ahead afraid his facial expression would reveal everything.

She continued. 'There was never any confusion about ownership. This is about doing the right thing and that would have been us sharing in the pleasure of seeing the finished pieces together before everyone else. Didn't I deserve that?'

Fuck. Arlo pulled up to the curb outside his brother's apartment. Silvia exited and slammed the door shut.

***

Arlo followed her up the stairs. At the top the door flung open to reveal his brother and girlfriend.

'So good to see you, man!' Luis slapped him on the back and pulled him in for a man-hug.

Luis was shorter than Arlo, with a pierced right ear and a tattoo peeking out of the sleeve of his T-shirt.

'Luis, this is Silvia. She works in our Tossa store. Silvia, this is Luis and Isabel.'

They showered her with kisses and greetings and ushered them both inside.

Arlo didn't miss the pair exchange a curious glance as they entered. Drinks were handed out and small talk commenced. Each time Arlo stood near Silvia she moved one step away. Luis and Isabel wanted to know about Australia as they were keen to travel there.

'It's so big. Do you think we'd see much in two weeks?'

Silvia laughed. 'Two weeks? Um, no, not much. It's a ten-hour drive between Sydney and Brisbane alone. You might be best picking one place you really want to visit and focus on that and see how much ground you can cover.'

'How far is Uluru?'

'Uluru is miles from anywhere. Do you think you could go for a bit longer? Maybe even a month? That way you could explore the east coast and see Melbourne and Sydney and hopefully Brisbane. You might not get as far as the Great Barrier Reef though.'

Her comments squashed their excitement. Isabel served dinner on the balcony.

'Is Eloisa still living in your apartment?' Luis asked Arlo after they'd taken their seats.

Arlo paused and crossed his ankles under the table, watched Silvia lift her wine glass and sip as she gazed out over the roof tops of Barcelona.

'Yes, she's looking for her own place but hasn't found anything yet.'

'She's got a new film out. It's been a while in between—'

Arlo tugged on the collar he wasn't wearing as the air became cloistered and thick.

'I haven't seen it.'

'The ads are everywhere. Have you been hiding down there in Tossa de Mar? Not living in the real world?' Isabel joked but it fell flat and Arlo didn't crack a smile.

'I no longer follow her career.'

'What? But I thought she was still lined up to wear the jewels on the red carpet for the movie premiere. Isn't that in a few weeks here in Barcelona? Or is it Madrid?'

'Silvia, that's Eloisa in the far photograph wearing special edition Blanco jewellery made especially for her,' Isabel said.

After a pause Silvia turned and glanced down the hall and faced them once more, without uttering a word.

Arlo shook his head. 'No, the pieces were made for the film.'

'Who is she?' Silvia's voice wavered as if she didn't really want to know.

Stillness came over the table. Arlo, his brother, and Isabel exchanged glances. Isabel frowned. Luis placed his hand over Isabel's intimating she should shut up.

Double fuck. This day was getting worse.

'Eloisa Mercedes is my wife. She is an American actress who has modelled our jewels on the red carpet when she's premiering a movie.'

'Your wife?'

Arlo turned in his seat and faced Silvia but she refused to do the same.

'We've been separated for over twelve months but we aren't yet divorced. She is still living in my apartment here in Barcelona which is why we couldn't stay there. I'm waiting for her to move out.'

He rarely saw Silvia mute. In fact, most of the time she had a lot to say. Her head was bowed seemingly lost in thought, until she rose and her chair scraped.

'Luis, Isabel, thank you so much for dinner. It was lovely to meet you. Can you please excuse me?'

Arlo covered his forehead with his arm at the sound of his mobile trilling. When it didn't stop, he opened one lid to find the bedroom dim with the soft light of dawn. He reached for the phone on the bedside table and squinted at the screen.

His father. His head crashed back against the pillow. There couldn't be a worse start to the day.

He cleared his throat and answered. '*Papa.*'

Ramon's voice was loud. No pleasantries, but that wasn't unusual, his father rambled on not taking a breath. Arlo sank back into the comfort of the bed until the diatribe couldn't be ignored, and the comment of *what the hell is going on* shouted, had him sitting bolt upright.

'*Papa*,' he repeated until he could get a word in.

'No, I didn't tell anyone about the new design. I wasn't even sure I'd present it until a few days ago. But when I saw it, I knew it was special and needed to be at the show. It's outstanding. You've seen the press, everyone loves it.'

His father replied.

'No, I haven't checked the figures yet. It was only released yesterday and it's not even breakfast time yet.' Ramon kept interrupting. 'Yes, we are usually inundated with orders following a release but there's still time yet.'

Arlo held the phone away from his ear while his father lamented his business strategy and ability to run the company, then he hung up. Ramon was just pissed off he hadn't been consulted first.

Nonetheless, not the best start to the day and following on from the disaster of last night.

Silvia would see sense today, he was sure. She'd have calmed down and would understand that he was only doing what's best. Best for the business, yes, but there wasn't any prejudice to her, was there? And well, the omission about his wife; that was different. They were separated, what did it matter?

He'd fix it. Easy. Do what it took. A gift perhaps, a jewel of her own? Yes, that would help.

Silvia had retreated to the spare room after opting not to sleep with him last night. Keen to see her, he dressed and entered the living area. She sat with his brother and Isabel.

'Silvia,' he acknowledged her. 'I thought we'd head into HQ and catch up with the team that made the collection. We'll grab a coffee and get going. You ready?'

'No, sorry, I'm heading out for breakfast with Luis and Isabel.' She turned away and he was dismissed. The *Sagrada Familia* was visible through the open balcony doors with the historic old stone sparkling in the morning sun. Arlo didn't fight, simply let her go.

Hours later the return car trip was quiet and uncomfortable. Small talk didn't work, nor little gestures of humour or even the flowers, coffee and Swiss chocolate gifts he'd given her upon their departure. Luckily, he had another trick up his sleeve.

They had almost reached the seaside town of Loret de Mar when he pulled into a spot that he knew would impress Silvia with the panoramic ocean views and endless stretch of coastline, all from an outdoor dining deck. It was also some of the best Spanish tapas on this side of the country.

If anything was going to thaw the Arctic freeze between them, it would be this view and good food.

'Silvia, I'm very sorry.'

She yanked off her oversized sun hat. 'For what?'

'For not telling you that I'm married. But we are separated. I've been living in Tossa and Eloisa has been in Barcelona. My marriage is over and has been for some time.'

'You haven't been in Tossa de Mar over twelve months.'

'No. That's correct. I moved out of our apartment and stayed with a friend for a while before heading back to Tossa.'

'It's a rather significant fact that you failed to mention. You didn't think it was important?' Her voice quavered as if she was having trouble keeping herself under control.

'Actually, no. We've been getting to know each other and the issue simply hadn't come up. To be honest, I try to think about my failed marriage as little as possible.'

Arlo tried to cool his growing frustration. He didn't owe Silvia anything. Okay, maybe he should have mentioned a wife, but her reaction was over the top hostile. The stone-cold silence she'd administered since finding out was deadly.

The waiter arrived with the dishes he'd selected for them.

Small servings of olives and calamari, cured hams and fried pota-toes. Arlo dropped a green olive into his mouth.

'I will not be like my mother.'

'Your mother?' He tried to connect the dots. Silvia had rarely spoken of her mother. 'I'm separated—'

She cut him off. 'So was my father when he started a rela-tionship with my mother. He said he was separated from his wife of ten years and did not plan to return. That he loved my mother and wanted to be with her.'

Arlo knew where this was heading. 'But I am separated,' he emphasised the words, 'and will not be reconciling with Eloisa.'

'That's what they all say!' Silvia spat out the words. He'd never heard her raise her voice and the sound drew him back in his chair.

'Yes, you are right.'

'What?' she whispered.

'Men who cheat on their wives are liars and opportunists and most of the time they want the best of both worlds. A wife and stable family at home plus the excitement of fresh blood at their beck and call. I've seen it.'

Arlo looked down at the spread of food and was no longer hungry. Anger swirled in his stomach, rushing through his veins, making them pop. 'I am not like that, damn it!' The veracity of the words scared him. He lowered his voice and now sounded defeated. 'You may not believe me. Fuck, you hardly know me. But I can say unequivocally that I am not like those men. And do you know why? Because I watched my mother's anguish at being the wife, the second choice of my father. The forgotten mother who kept the house running and cared for the children, that cared for my father. She was relegated to the confines of the home that wasn't exciting to my father anymore. Who was surrounded by attractive women modelling the jewels he'd designed, pouring themselves over him and him being unable to resist their advances. Him not being man enough to love my mother and my mother alone. Who spent many nights out late, sometimes weekends and weeks away from his family and my mother's bed. My father was taught well by my grandfather.'

Silvia was silent. He'd revealed more than he wanted to. More than he intended.

'I'm sorry. That's horrible.'

He nodded unable to form any more words.

'My mother was the woman left behind because my father chose his wife and other children over her. Not me. I will not wait around for a man while he provides empty promises. I will not be second choice. My life is worth more than that.'

He couldn't argue with that. And he agreed. He would never leave a woman hanging like that, precarious and unsure. Not someone he cared about anyway. Despite everything, the situation he found himself in, he admired her. Silvia was not vulnerable nor a woman to be taken advantage of. She was strong.

Silvia rose, took one last glance at the view and walked away.

Their journey continued in silence. Now Arlo didn't feel like making it better, talking, trying to fix things. One thing he found hard to tolerate was being accused of something he wasn't. This womaniser tag had followed him his whole life. Yes, he played it up when it suited him, yes, he pretended to net the big deal, and sometimes he even liked it. But it was not who he was. He'd loved Eloisa and she'd left him for another man. So, no apologies, but from his point of view, this whole long-term commitment of love, well he didn't think too much of it.

They pulled up outside his house. Arlo reached over and touched her lower arm. He kept his head bowed when he spoke.

'Silvia. You are talented. You have a unique eye for detail and design and fresh and vibrant ideas. I don't think you realise it. What we've done together, it takes years to hone that craft. What we created is special. I think we can do it again.'

Silvia's hand had been on the door handle but she spun around in the passenger seat so fast her hair swirled around her shoulders. 'What? You want me to come up with another idea for you? You, who is all out of ideas, couldn't think of anything until I suggested the yellow design piece. You want me to do the legwork for you and then you take all the credit? So, your business can make another few million? You must think I'm stupid.'

His body temperature doubled and his blood boiled in his veins. Tugging at his collar, he tried to release some air, cool himself down. His hands fidgeted fighting the urge to punch something.

'It's the least you can do after what your grandmother did.'

Her mouth set firm and her eyes squinted in his direction.

'What are you insinuating?'

'Your grandmother was a thief. When she fled Spain, she stole the black spinel collection and the original designs to prevent them ever being made again.'

Silvia's eyes widened along with her mouth forming a perfect 'O'. Her fury was palpable, he could feel it radiating towards him in waves. Just as she was about to unleash it upon him, a knock came behind Arlo, onto the windowpane of the driver's door. Silvia's mouth shut.

Arlo flicked his head over his shoulder. Eloisa stood outside his car. No, it couldn't be. A lump formed in his throat. He blinked, but when he reopened his eyes, she remained standing there.

He bowed his head. Silvia yanked open the passenger door until it almost swung back and hit her. She shot out of the open space and escaped down his drive.

Arlo blew air out of his cheeks. What an arsehole. His words were cruel and unforgivable. The knowledge of it twisted and turned inside of him. Arlo lived by two rules. Never to be like his father and the second, never hurt a woman. He might struggle to believe in true love but he'd broken one of his own fundamental rules. That was a vow he'd made as he cuddled his mother as she cried silent tears night after night until her heart had hardened too. He'd attacked the one person Silvia truly loved. Not only was he a bastard, but he was a coward too.

He reluctantly left the confines of the car and Eloisa pulled him into an unwelcome embrace.

Chapter Twenty-One

The pencil flew across the page of Silvia's hardbacked notebook.

With each line and filigree, her heart rate slowed, her limbs loosened and she gradually fell into that other place: her creative space. Where all that mattered was the next stroke.

Once that happy place had been within the pages of a scientific journal and studying the intricacies of anatomy. Somehow her entire passion for medicine had disappeared over the last five years. She shook those thoughts away; she'd worry about that later, when she returned to real life in Australia. Only three weeks away. Which meant her return to medical school was imminent and not something she could ignore.

Ideas had been brewing since her visit to the jewellery convention and seeing the works of Gaudi. His minute detail fascinated her and added to that, his use of colour. Now those ideas were zooming out of her pencil; she could hardly keep up, but it was calming and methodical, and exactly what she needed.

Would Arlo like this? She banished the thought. He could go to hell. He'd never see the ideas she'd scribbled in this book. This was her special design pad; the one Paloma had gifted her. She curled her fingers in and out to the shape of a fist and flicked back through the pages until she found it.

The black spinel was the very first. Silvia skimmed back and forth between the more recent drawings by Paloma and this one. Her eyes widened. The strokes were similar, but mixed in with those were more hard, deep and rough edges, as if someone else had added their touch. She'd always thought they were her grandmother's drawings, hence why she had the book. But if Paloma had drawn these designs, or at the very least, been part of their production, how could she be a thief?

Silvia's pencil stalled in her hand. With a dreaded, sinking sensation, she realised the worst conclusion. Paloma *must* have assisted Carlo, but regardless, the pieces were Blanco. She might have argued with Arlo about her role in designing the Silvia set, but she'd been clear about ownership. They were never her pieces. Arlo said the black spinel set was stolen. But the question remained—did Paloma steal them or were they secretly gifted?

Silvia knew her granny. If she had taken them, it would never have been a whim, it would have been a deliberate act. Was it revenge or simply taking what she sincerely thought was hers?

What a mess! And the worst part was she may never know the truth.

Going to the back of the book, she looked over the last design drawn by Paloma and a shooting pain cracked through Silvia's chest. Her grandmother was ailing near the end, but she had refused to stop. Her wrinkled and long and slender fingers had shaken as she gripped both the pencil and the page too tightly.

Silvia's eyes pooled with tears as she gazed at that last image. It was poignant, original and not in any way garish or vulgar like the *Maison de Bijoux* collection. The inspiration had been simple. Her grandmother had extracted a twig from the garden; it was long and slim and had small leaves protruding from each side and had smelled divine, sharp and tangy. Paloma had drawn a bangle that copied the shape of the sprig. A streak of gold had turned into a long plentiful leaf twirling and overlapping. As a last thought, she'd placed exquisite, tiny green gems at regular intervals along the face, the gold contrasting with the verdant green.

Silvia returned to what she'd just drawn. It was so different to her grandmother's sweet, simple pieces. This creation jumped off the page and wasn't subtle. But Gaudi wasn't simple, either. The colours alone made an impact. Sort of like an abstract painting.

Was her grandmother a designer too? Silvia sensed heartache had caused her to stop jewellery design and making. And that was why later in life, she was able to revisit it with her grand-daughter. Did Silvia have the talent of her untrained grand-mother? Was Arlo right?

This new idea was bold, chunky not delicate or fine. It had layers upon layers of metal with bright gemstones. It was like nothing she'd ever worn or hankered for or even desired to make. Elegance and beauty had always been her objective. Not making a statement.

Perhaps it was reflective of her mood.

Did Arlo's wife wear jewellery like this? Did she make statements? She was an American actress after all.

Silvia placed the book facedown and scrolled upwards on the screen of her phone and entered the search term *Eloisa Mercedes*. Was that even her real name? Sounded like a stage name.

The screen exploded with hits. Glamorous shots on red carpets, at the beach in a bikini, art galleries, cake stalls, fancy balls. In every single photo she looked amazing. How was that even possible? Didn't the woman have a bad hair day?

No doubt about it, Eloisa was gorgeous in all her blonde and white beauty. Whereas Arlo was dark, she was all creams and lightness. Pale skin that sparkled, fluorescent teeth that bounced off the page, and always the elegant frocks. Dresses were too ordinary a word for the clothes she wore.

A listing of her films came up next. She'd appeared in some American blockbusters, those action sort that Silvia never watched. The ones that usually featured a brawny male actor with a machine gun at his belt. She kept scrolling and inevitably came across social pages. At some point Arlo and Eloisa had been a popular couple with their images emblazoned across every gossip magazine.

Silvia's heart skipped a beat as she gazed at the dark and handsome man. When she'd arrived in Spain, she'd considered a holiday fling. Is that what she was doing? It didn't feel like that anymore. A weight pressed on her chest. Without her noticing the thing she had with Arlo had morphed into something else.

Stupid, Silvia. Your own fault. What did you think would happen? You'd have sex with the Lothario of Tossa and he'd fall madly in love with you and move to Australia?

She gazed at the photo again; he appeared happy, younger, his hair longer. No scowl. They made the perfect couple.

If Arlo didn't love Eloisa, why keep her a secret?

But the answer to that was simple, she didn't know him.

A thought came to her.

'Silvia!' Her name being called sounded like a long way away. It rang out again. Esmeralda?

She left her bedroom and entered the loungeroom of the apartment. Esmeralda was putting away groceries and bottles before wiping down benches and tidying up.

She watched Esmeralda, part of her only remaining family and Silvia lost it. A rush of tears rolled down her face followed by sobs she couldn't hold in. Esmeralda dropped the sponge and rushed forwards to embrace her and mop at her cheeks with a tissue before leading her to the sofa and forcing her to sit. She rushed away and returned with an espresso for each of them.

'What's wrong my love? No, wait. I'll show you some photographs first.' Esmeralda fished them out of her bag and placed a small pile on Silvia's lap.

On top was a photograph of a young Paloma outside the Pink Poodle. Silvia cried harder.

Paloma was tall and slender and had a pulled back wave-style. Very sixties. Her clothes were pastel hues. In some images she stood alone, others with family members. Then there was a collection of her in different locations around Tossa.

She held one up closer to see who her grandmother was photographed with.

'Is that Carlo Blanco? And is that outside the store in town?'

Esmeralda tightened her lips and her features became squashed like she'd tasted something unpleasant.

'Yes. The rest of these are of Carlo. Some by himself. Silvia, this is evidence that something was going on between them. He was her boss. And it was the sixties remember. Maybe now in these modern times, you might socialise with your employer, but not alone and not with a married man and her being a young impressionable girl. Even the simple number of photographs of them together raises questions. See here. They are at the beach, the markets, visiting friends, having dinner, some at the store. Even if you didn't want to believe anything untoward, there's this one.' Without explaining, she handed it to Silvia.

Paloma and Carlo were entwined in an embrace and kissing.

'I think you're right,' Silvia put the photos down. 'Arlo said something about his father and his grandfather both cheating on their wives. He said it was common but that doesn't mean Paloma did anything wrong.'

'That's right!' Esmeralda's exclamation was fierce. Then she calmed and swallowed the remainder of her coffee in one gulp. 'Nothing other than falling in love with a married man who may have taken advantage of her.'

'I think she really loved him. Even if it was wrong and he had a family.'

'I wonder what happened to drive her so far away from us?' Esmeralda pondered.

'Other than he perhaps found someone new or grew bored? That is what happens with these illicit affairs. Maybe Valencia found out and he had to call it off?'

'There's something else. Just wait a second.' Silvia raced to her room and returned as quickly as possible.

'This is the full set of jewellery.' Silvia repeated how special it was to her grandmother and today Esmeralda exclaimed at its beauty.

'Even though she loved jewellery, she didn't wear any, except a couple of pieces I made for her over the years at school, but that was cheap sentimental stuff. Often, when we'd draw together, she'd have this faraway look in her eyes as if she was dreaming of somewhere else.'

Silvia let the words sink in.

'Arlo said...'

'Oh, yes, Arlo. Have you been spending time together? He seems lovely.'

'What? I thought you hated the Blanco family?'

'Y-e-s, but that was about his grandfather. Arlo is so good-looking and nice. He helped us.' She turned and faced Silvia now. 'Carlo is a grub and he did no good by our Paloma, I'm sure of it.' She kissed her fingers and raised them towards the sky. 'Oh, but Arlo, he's different.' Her aunt swooned, batted her eyelids and made a gooey smile.

Esmeralda was loving on Arlo just as she was hating him. Surprising, he must have worked some magic after the boat disaster. But bugger, it created a dilemma for Silvia. What would she reveal about Arlo's view of Paloma? Could Silvia reveal the Blanco family thought her sister was a thief? No, she couldn't. Silvia shut her mouth. The accusations would hurt her aunt, not to mention make her furious, and just when the generation old feud was thawing.

'Now pack up your things, let's go. You're coming home for dinner with me. I'm making my famous spicy chorizo and eggplant paella. You'll love it.'

Silvia was sure food wouldn't solve her problems, but spending time with her loud and vivacious family, might.

Chapter Twenty-Two

'What are you doing here?'

'To say hi?' Eloisa said.

'Your timing is impeccable.' Arlo looked over his shoulder and along the drive but Silvia was out of sight.

'Ah, lover's tiff?'

Arlo wouldn't dignify the comment with a response. 'What can I do for you, Eloisa?'

'Well, it's what I can do for you.'

He doubted that. 'What can you do for me then?' He didn't love her anymore but what was the point in remaining bitter? At the time, Arlo's world had collapsed. Less than two years after they married, Eloisa announced not only that she was pregnant but the baby belonged to the last lead actor in her multi-million dollar film and she was moving in with him.

Even hard-nosed Arlo had found that hard to take. But the old cliché was right, time healed wounds.

'I'm here to offer my services. My representation of your business stopped when we separated.'

Something about her tone was off. He considered his ex-wife; she looked older, less immaculately dressed than usual but it was her agitated movements that struck him as odd.

'Let's go into the house.' He let her lead the way. Eloisa stumbled up the few short steps and had to hold onto the railing for support. Arlo opened the door and Gus rushed forward ready for play. He pounced on Eloisa and she crashed backwards onto her bottom. He grabbed Gus by the collar and held him in place. The dog licked his face and hands. He gave the dog attention before reaching out and offering his hand to help her.

She was lighter than he remembered. Her arm in his grip felt like a matchstick. The sleeve of her dress had rolled up revealing a patchwork quilt of scars. Aware his eyes were upon her bare skin, she pushed down the cloth of her dress.

Alarm bells rang. Something was going on. 'Come through to the kitchen and I'll make a drink.'

Arlo busied himself with his back to Eloisa and didn't make conversation. He placed two steaming mugs on the bench and sat across from her at the kitchen island.

'This is different. Since when do you drink tea?' Her words dripped with sarcasm and she wore a grin.

He shrugged. 'I hear you have a new movie out?'

Eloisa sipped her tea, grimaced and put it back down, nodded. 'Can I have something stronger?'

'Are you still with whatshisface?'

'Yes, and his name is Cameron.' Eloisa proceeded to sing his praises about his success as a movie star in Hollywood.

'Why aren't you with him now and why do you need money?'

Her eyes narrowed and she sat up taller. 'He's on location in Guatemala. Nothing for me to do there and there's no spot for me on that film. I'm back home for a while. And why do you think I need money?'

'Eloisa, there's no chance you'd want to do a showcase for *Blanco Fine Jewels* if life was going well. You didn't want to be associated with the business when we were married. You liked the jewels, though, but who wouldn't?'

She sneered and diverted attention, looking around the house. 'This place always was spectacular. Pity it's located in a nothing-bit town.'

'Look, I've got things to do and we can go on like this all day. Why do you need money?'

Eloisa walked to the French doors overlooking the vista and sauntered back to sit on the stool. She lifted her arm and in a clumsy gesture knocked over the hot tea, the liquid covering the bench.

Arlo jumped up and grabbed the nearest cloth. Eloisa didn't move at the trickle of hot liquid dripping onto her dress. He cleaned up and tossed the dirty cloth back into the sink before standing next to Eloisa and holding her chin in his hand.

Her eyes were streaked red, the whites dim. Her pupils were dilated into large circles. He roughly shoved up both sleeves and examined her arms.

'Are you on drugs?'

Eloisa reefed her arms back out of his grip and laughed.

'Well, I would be if that loser would give me some more money. I can't pay for drugs if I don't have the cash. He's in

Central America buying his stash dirt-cheap. He's left me with none.' Her arms shook with the effort of speaking. But in the same instant her eyelids drooped.

In one swoop Arlo picked up Eloisa and carried her upstairs to the spare bedroom. He tucked her in like a child, left her a glass of water and went to his study. He had loads of work to do but if he didn't help her, who would? However, he didn't think she wanted the help he was prepared to give.

Over the next few hours, he spoke on the telephone to various drug rehabilitation centres within a one-hundred-kilometre radius until he found a vacancy. It cost a fortune. Eloisa could afford the fee if she sold the remaining Blanco pieces she owned. But Arlo would never force her to do that. A hard enough road lay ahead.

The late afternoon sun had a penetrating orange glow. He sat on the deck where only a few days ago he'd been making passionate love to Silvia. He poured himself a double scotch on the rocks, wishing she was next to him enjoying her own drink. Now he had to sort out his wife. First thing in the morning he'd admit her to the rehab centre. He didn't know what her addictions were. But he wasn't one of them.

Silvia hardly slept.

After hours of contemplation, she wanted to discuss the mystery of her grandmother with Arlo. Like her family, his relatives had strong views on the shared history. Each family held their alliances close to their own, neither considering the worst of their own tribe but comfortable blaming others.

And what about her and Arlo? That was harder. If he had used her for a new design, well, he'd won. But that was over, the *Silvia collection* had been released. Did that mean they were over? And what exactly was it that might be over? She wasn't stupid enough to consider it a relationship; she might have to accept a holiday romance. But was there more between them?

She needed answers, so as soon as the dawn sun penetrated her curtains, she rose and headed out to her favourite spot in Tossa for yoga, the tranquil cove to the rear of the castle.

Clarity of thought descended during the workout. As Silvia walked home to dump her gear and change, her muscles ached but her steps were lighter because she had a plan. She'd surprised herself at how quickly she'd adjusted to life in Spain. Those first few weeks she'd been a fish out of water, uncomfortable, yet amazed at the coastal town. Now she walked the narrow and bustling streets with confidence; knew where to buy her fresh vegies and emergency supplies from the local chemist. Knew the best places to eat and the exact spot on the beach to avoid the summer crowd.

Now the end of June, summer had struck with force and the days were balmy, so much it felt like home. Sweat beads rolled down the dip in her chest as she walked the slight rise to Arlo's mansion.

Rounding the bend in the road, she watched the metallic blue Mercedes Benz reverse out of his garage. Acting on instinct, Silvia moved behind a copse of trees lining the road. She crouched low and held one narrow trunk for support. Arlo drove by with his wife in the passenger seat.

She let the car pass and rose, brushing away leaves and detritus, wiping away her embarrassment. She had her answer. Silvia stood there gripping the branch catching the breath that the scene had stolen away. An ache commenced in her chest and spread through her torso and breastbone leaving in its wake a hole. That sense of being alone once more washed over her and embraced her like a cloak, suffocating and snatching away any coherent thought.

After her grandmother died, she was lonely. That had made her decision to fulfil her dying grandmother's wish so easy. And a distraction.

Then her arrival in Spain had been consumed with Arlo's company. Something she'd loved and enjoyed and had meant little time to dwell on her grief. She bent over, hands resting on her knees. Damn it, she'd come to rely upon him but again, here she was alone. Her trip had been her permission to start living again, but now she felt empty inside. She'd been an idiot.

Perhaps it was time to go home.

The process was a rigmarole. Not helped by the fact that Eloisa changed her mind upon entry to the rehab centre and refused to stay. A scene had ensued and many hours passed but now Arlo headed back into Tossa de Mar.

The twinkling lights provided comfort. He was getting used to this being his permanent abode. Could he live here full time?

Didn't matter how tired he was, he needed to find Silvia. He was confident she'd understand about Eloisa, it was the history involving her grandmother that might prove more difficult to smooth over. Arlo needed to apologise for the harsh things he'd said in the heat of the moment. Yes, he believed Paloma took the jewellery but he had no evidence and he had to accept that. They'd have to agree that the precise history was unknown and reach a truce of sorts.

Her mobile rang unanswered. Arlo went to the apartment and no one responded to his knock. Damn it. This wasn't part of the plan. He knocked again, pounding on the door.

'Hey, mate, what's up?' A tall, dark male opened the door.

Arlo pushed past him and into the entry, 'Silvia! Silvia!'

He searched the rooms until he found her, the last one in the corner. Clothes were strewn over the bed and floor, a suitcase sitting open and half-packed.

'No, you can't leave.'

'Silvia, who's this dude?' Leo stood at the bedroom door.

'It's okay, Leo. This is Arlo.'

Leo threw a look of disdain in their direction before leaving.

'Please, stop.' He snatched a cardigan from her hands and threw it on the bed. 'Can we please talk.'

'You are incredibly rude.'

'I said please.'

Arlo watched as she completed folding a T-shirt before placing it in the case. Then she folded her arms across her chest.

'Silvia, look at me.' He reached for her wrists and tugged her close until she faced him. 'We need to talk. I'm sorry for the things I said, they came out wrong.' There was no protest from her so he continued, gently drawing her down to sit on the bed.

'I don't know what happened in the past and I don't know whose fault it was. But I know you loved your grandmother and she was the only parent you had.'

Silvia jumped in, interrupting his chain of thought. 'I know, Arlo, I'm so sorry. We don't know what happened. My family defends my grandmother as I'm inclined to do and your family defends the business and your grandfather—'

'They don't defend my grandfather; they simply don't talk of it. But the family know about the jewellery and say after it was designed, the set was never seen again and my grandfather refused to talk about it and it was never recreated.'

'Do you think Paloma and Carlo were having an affair?'

Arlo looked out the open sliding glass doors and away, his gaze cast upon the far horizon.

'My family is convinced something was going on, that it ended badly and that's when Paloma fled Spain. It does seem coincidental,' she said.

Arlo collected his thoughts. 'It's likely. The undisputed facts are that she worked in the store with Carlo. It appeared as if she had an interest and maybe a talent for jewels and design. This ironic sense of *déjà vu* is not lost on me, I can assure you. Once I was aware of not only your interest, but your talent, I was drawn to spend time with you. It naturally evolved, by agreement, that you spent the evenings assisting me.' He reached out and held her hands. 'I needed you, it's true. You reignited my creativity and self-belief. I couldn't have made the Silvia Collection without you.' He paused, cast his gaze down at their hands. 'I can imagine how it may have played out all those years ago. I'm sure you can too. But what we must do this time, is ensure the ending is different. I am nothing like my father or my grandfather.'

'Who do you think designed those black spinal pieces?' asked Silvia.

'I think if they had only been my grandfather's idea, without any input from Paloma, he would have reproduced them. But he didn't and insisted no one else do so either. That leads to a conclusion he was mad, so spurned, they were something he couldn't consider revisiting. Carlo was a tough man. He would have had his reasons.'

'I hope the reason is that he loved my grandmother like I think she did him. I hope it was an ill-fated grand love affair.'

'Maybe that's true. After all, he didn't peruse the pieces or seek any form of recrimination. And that would have been something he would have done without a trace of guilt in other circumstances.'

'Arlo, you might be right. Regardless, if Paloma took the jewellery, she would have had a good reason. Maybe they were sentimental, maybe he even let her? We don't know.'

'We don't know,' he agreed.

'I'm sorry if she took them unlawfully. But I can't apologise for something that must have felt right to her in the circumstances, at the time.'

Silvia got up and retrieved the set and opened the box. 'You should have them back.' And she tried to hand over the case.

'No, absolutely not.' He held up his hands. 'They were precious to your grandmother and they are precious to you. They belong with you.'

A single tear rolled down Silvia's cheek. Arlo placed the pad of his thumb to her face and brushed it away.

'You said you want to rewrite the ending this time? But like your grandfather, you are married. Where's Eloisa?'

'I dropped her to a drug rehabilitation program this morning. She needs help and now she's getting it. Plus, she's agreed to divorce. I'll get my lawyers onto that straight away.'

'You don't love her?'

'No,' he bowed his head. 'I did. I loved her with all my heart and she betrayed me. Did the one thing I cannot tolerate. Honesty and trust are everything. I have seen the damage lies cause in relationships and the heartache when there is not total commitment between two people.'

'She cheated on you?'

Arlo told her the story.

'I think I love you, Silvia.'

Silvia laughed. Not the reaction he was hoping for.

'You sure know how to woo a girl. You think you love me?'

He cracked a smile. Her taunt was teasing. 'I always protect myself, even now. Silvia, you are the most intelligent and kind woman I've ever met. You are smart but do not make people feel dumb in your presence; you are generous with your time and helpful to others without seeking a benefit in return; and you've restored my faith in people. You are a good person and they do exist in this shamelessly shallow world we live in. Plus, you are the most beautiful woman I've had the pleasure of spending time with.' He wasn't finished. 'But what I find the most attractive is your passion. You have the passion for jewels like me. I've finally found a match. You experience that special excitement at an idea, at the prospect of creating something beautiful, I see it in you. But you also have the talent of knowing what will work, how pieces fit together, what gives a wow factor but is also practical enough to wear. It's rare that anyone matches my enthusiasm and passion for jewels. You are a talented designer and have an eye for detail that's unique.'

'You forgot a few things. I'm poor and you're mega-rich, I'm Australian and you live in Spain.' Her features turned pensive.

'Do you only think you love me because we can design incredible jewellery together?'

'Silvia, you have Spanish blood in your veins.' He tried to lighten the moment but found he didn't want to. 'I want a relationship with all of the usual things including an ability for us to create together. You mean so much more to me than just the jewels.'

'I can only tell you how I feel. I haven't been able to stop thinking about you since that night at the party. When I'm not with you, I want to be. You are strong and confident and take what you want. And bloody hell, James Bond good-looking with your suits and fancy cars. But I know, underneath there's so much more to you than this alpha-macho image that the girls fall for. You're like the cliché, a tough guy but really a big soft teddy bear. And I've seen your ability to care and love . . . it's admirable. But most of all, you're loyal and I know you would never hurt me.'

'Let's not get carried away, there's nothing soft about me.' He tapped his stomach holding it taut. 'I've had very bad teachers and my vow was to be a different man, a better man than the ones in my life. But I do believe we could be a great team. We are both driven by the same passion—to make beautiful jewellery.'

'And how would your family feel about that?'

'How would your family react?' he responded with the same question.

'Well, lucky you saved my family that day on the boat because there's been a thaw. At least with Esmeralda, she now thinks you're "lovely".' Silvia gestured with her fingers.

He smiled. 'I'm glad to hear it. My mother would love you.

My father doesn't love anyone but once he becomes aware of your talent, then he will admire you and respect you and no doubt try to take advantage of you.'

Silvia leaned back. Arlo moved forward, 'Oh no, I'm sorry, I don't mean it like that. He will want to exploit your ability to make fine jewels. But he will also notice how attractive you are.'

Silvia shuddered.

'I'm not going to be relegated to the shopfront for ever?'

Laughing, he moved closer. 'You can do whatever you want. But I think your talent lies in design.'

'Far out, Arlo. I'm going to be a doctor.'

He lowered his head.

'It's a dream I've had forever. Plus, I live in Australia!' She looked out over the distance, at the expansive blue ocean and she knew she couldn't leave him. Grabbing the hem of his shirt, she tugged him towards her. 'I have nothing left for me at home anyway. And if I'm honest, I haven't wanted to return to med school—'

'If you want it, we can make it happen? Part-time design and university?'

Silvia didn't want those things anymore, but she was glad he was prepared to offer them. 'Remember the yellow diamond set? Don't ever do that to me again. It was ours and we make the decisions together. Lucky, I think I love you, too, so I forgive you this once.' She smiled wickedly. 'Can we work out the details later...' and her words trailed away as they kissed.

Chapter Twenty-Three

Standing at the bow of the *Valencia*, the Costa Brava had never looked more beautiful to Silvia.

Spain was different to where she grew up, with the green rolling hills, roosters crowing in the early hours and organic fresh produce on every corner. Here, the sand was golden, the ocean all shades of azure-blue with white tips, the sun warm and the lifestyle hospitable.

This country had gotten under her skin and while she might not call it home, it stirred something within her. Equal measures of excitement and a contentment she hadn't experienced before. Not a shred of loneliness.

Her love for the town and area had grown, of course, with her love for Arlo, but also her extended family. This place had a wonderful ability to connect people. And the Garcia family had embraced this young Australian girl as one of their own. She had achieved what she wanted. To feel closer to Paloma, visit her beloved homeland and connect with the places of her childhood.

Admittedly, the image of the loving grandmother she'd had when she arrived in Spain had changed and having learned so much more about her as a young woman and what she may have faced, made Silvia love her even more.

She might never be sure of the nature of Paloma's relationship with Carlo Blanco but she was sure that her grandmother had loved Joe. Whether he'd been convenient at the time didn't matter. For many years she'd lived amongst their love. It was real. And a love she was keen to recreate. No one could deter her otherwise. If Paloma had fled after her heart was broken, and taken what she thought was hers, or maybe even, what she knew wasn't, well, that was in the past.

Her grandmother's early life had brought Silvia to *Blanco Fine Jewels* and that meant to Arlo. Two generations later, like her, Arlo and Silvia were linked, across countries and around the globe.

She'd thought of Joe over the last few hours. She'd loved her grandfather and didn't want to forget him. Maybe she would finish her medical degree one day but she knew, finally accepted, that she wasn't that person anymore. Perhaps her unconditional love for him had steered her direction when she didn't have one. Maybe her lack of a father figure had endeared Joe to her even more. How else had she so easily walked away from medicine all those years ago? Silvia knew she could have dropped to part-time status at uni; they would have given her special dispensation. But she hadn't, instead she'd walked away to care for Paloma. She'd quickly forgotten about the endless nights of study and losing herself in textbooks and the anatomy of body parts. Those choices led her here.

It was a day of reckoning.

Today she was finally putting her grandmother to rest in the Mediterranean Sea that she'd loved so much.

On board were both the Blanco and Garcia families. What family feud? It was like it had never happened. Esmeralda chatted with Arlo's family and had them in stitches with funny tales of people she knew, places she'd been or simply her shopping trip that day. For Silvia, the hardest part was warming to Ramon, Arlo's father. Particularly when his mother Valencia was such a beautiful woman. A real stalwart of the family. She loved the affection between Arlo and his mother but she knew he tried to make up for the shortcomings of his father. And it was the fatal flaw of the Blanco men that had made Arlo the man he was: loyal and trustworthy and someone who worshipped her, loved her like a goddess.

He'd helped her realise she wasn't like her own mother; she had greater strength of conviction. But her mother had been strong. Again, the past wasn't present to reveal its secrets. She'd never know if her mother had sat in wait for her father to return. She hoped not. But she had been tough. To raise a child alone, to remain alone and to have her life cut short. A tragedy. But Silvia was different.

She heard Arlo release the throttle and reduce the speed of the boat. Holding the railing she walked back into the cabin while he stalled the boat and lowered the anchor.

'What do you think about here?'

They were surrounded by blue ocean on every side. The land a distant view off the rear. The water was pure and deep and stretched both up and down the coastline and beyond.

'Perfect.' She wrapped her arms around him. Touching him at any time she liked still provided her with a thrill that ran straight up her spine. Arlo was strong against her, his body firm. He made her feel strong. She knew she could achieve anything with him by her side. Tears welled in her eyes, but this was a happy moment. Knowing her grandmother was where she loved most in the world was special.

Arlo moved away and gathered the families together. No words would be spoken. It had all been said. When the group was gathered, she poured the ashes from the china urn into the sea. Arlo stood beside her and always, Esmeralda's force nearby; Paloma's dearest sister who sobbed. But those tears were more about long-lost dreams and old memories.

'Let's celebrate,' Cruz announced as only the Spanish would. Happy or sad occasions were marked with endless merriment. There was lots of food and drink on board. This time no half-naked bikini clad women, probably to his disappointment.

A not unpleasant burden lifted from Silvia. She'd fulfilled her promise and contentment grew inside of her, like a flower blossoming. She hadn't realised that she'd been holding tight to this important task, and it had been coiling inside of her, tightening as the days passed. Now it unfurled and she felt lighter.

Leo brought her a plate of food. Fresh seafood, salad and bread. 'I guess there's no chance for me now?' He asked, his face deadpan and serious.

Silvia leaned in close so only he could hear. 'There was never any chance.'

'No?' he questioned.

'No.'

'Okay, well, *salud*,' and he held up his bottle of local beer and offered cheers. Silvia smiled then and returned the gesture.

Cruz joined them. 'Well, cuz, what a trip, hey? What now? How are you and lover boy going to manage?'

Silvia finished munching on her mouthful of food. 'It's early days. But I've accepted a position with the business. Can you believe it?' Her grin covered her whole face. 'Who would have thought this would have occurred all those weeks ago when I rocked up on your doorstep.'

'Not me for sure,' Cruz responded.

'I have to go home and tidy up a few things, rent out the house and get organised. Arlo is going to come with me. He's excited about going to Australia for the first time.'

'You are going to move here?'

'Not sure. We think we'll live here for the summer and perhaps live in Australia over your winter which will be our summer at home in the southern hemisphere.'

'Weird,' Leo contributed.

'Who knows? I'm taking one day at a time.'

Arlo joined them along with Esmeralda and Valencia. She was surrounded by these older, wise women. Just like Paloma had been. They would never replace her grandmother but she felt enormously comforted by their presence.

Valencia leaned over and touched her knee. 'I am so excited to see you two together. Arlo has done nothing but work, work, work and now he might have a different focus. Have some fun. Or maybe there will be little bambinos to make us feel young again.'

Arlo choked on his food that turned into a laugh when he recovered.

'It will still be about business, Mama,' he said but smiled. 'We are going to be especially busy if Silvia keeps designing best-sellers.' It was to their delight, and of course, Ramon's and the business executive, that the Silvia Collection had been in high demand, so far, one of the top buys. Business was once again booming. 'It's going to be a very exciting future.'

'What do you think your grandmother would say about your working for Blanco?' Valencia asked.

Silvia paused and everyone waited on her answer. 'I think she would love it. She'd be proud and a little bit reminiscent of what might have been for her.'

'Hear, hear,' Esmeralda sang.

Hours later after the boat had emptied of family, Silvia looked through her design book, flipping the pages slowly. What had once been her grandmother's history, was now shared.

Arlo poured them both a drink and sat beside her.

'The first time I knew about this book, I wanted to steal it away from you. I was so desperate to save the business that I would have done anything.'

Instead of responding to his admission, she said, 'I think we should recreate the black spinel collection.' She let him absorb her words.

'Really?' he questioned.

'Yes. Perhaps not identical, we can put a fresh twist on it. But use the gems. We can't let them be taboo forever. And maybe we can name it after my grandmother. What do you think?'

He leaned in and kissed her. With his forehead touching hers, he said, 'A fabulous idea.'

Silvia kept turning the pages.

Arlo reached out and made her pause. 'What's this?'

'I drew these after our Barcelona weekend. I was inspired by Gaudi.' She looked up at him and saw the awe in his face.

'Silvia, these are incredible. The colours, the shapes, everything. You are amazing. What else do you have hiding in this remarkable book?'

Silvia tapped her temples indicating her creating was in her head. But she laughed and tossed her hair over her shoulder. Her eyes sparkled with mischief. 'And, that my love is exactly why I'll keep creating for you. If you give me reactions like that every time, how can I resist?'

'I'll show you my love in other ways, too.' Arlo let his hand sit at the meeting of her legs. She wore a short summer dress and her legs were bare. Silvia reached up and cupped his face, the stubble rough on her fingers. They kissed deeply, not the fervent urgent clashes of lips and tongues like their first exchange but rather slow, deliberate and tantalising with the knowledge that there were plenty more to come.

'I've got a brilliant idea. Let's sail to Monte Carlo. We can leave now,' he said as he nuzzled her neck. 'Or maybe in a few minutes after we've gotten reacquainted.'

Silvia laughed as his hands swooped under her and slipped her down the bench seat. 'I could get used to life with you.' And she returned his kiss and relished the feel of his strong hand over her thigh before it rose higher. She shivered in anticipation and not just at the thought of loving Arlo but of the life she had ahead of her. She curled her body up to meet his and the bracelet jingled on her arm.

Her grandmother, forever close.

Acknowledgments

This is a new series and I'm a bit nervous about it because it's a departure from my Australian settings, plus it has the millionaire trope. I hope that if you've read it, you'll see it still contains my signature style and the only real difference is that I'm transporting you to exotic and beautiful destinations around the world. And one of the main characters happens to be very wealthy! This book series was born out of COVID and my desire to armchair travel when we couldn't.

Adding to that was the need to escape, be free and whisked away. Plus, I had been thinking for some time about writing a story with jewels (I'm a little obsessed with Tiffany) and that led to millionaires and the world they inhabit. It was so much fun to imagine their rich and luxurious lifestyles and it added such a wonderful layer of glamour to the novels. And rest assured, I'll continue to write my Australian based stories, but perhaps there'll be another series with overseas locations in the future, too!

I'd like to thank my early readers, Leigh and Mary-Lou for their insight and help on the early drafts. Thank you to Annie Seaton for her wonderful editing skills and for making my words shine, and to EJP Covers for the gorgeous cover. And, as always, thank you for reading, I hope that if you enjoyed this one, you'll pick up the next book in the series. I also hope that reading The Spanish Jeweller allowed you to escape whatever it is you wanted to get away from, for just a few short hours. Let me know if it worked for you.

About the Author

Leanne Lovegrove is a lawyer, wife and mother and a lover of romance and reading. Her law career created an addiction to coffee but provides countless story ideas. She is the author of romantic fiction. Leanne writes sweeping love stories with happily-ever-afters with strong female heroines and often set in the beautiful landscape of Australia. This is her first book in her European Tycoon series. This time she has left the shores of Australia behind for the exotic climes of various European cities for romances with dashing Tycoons. She lives in Brisbane, Australia with her husband and three children.

Other books in the European Tycoon series

The French Perfumer (European Tycoons #2)
Available for Pre-order

The Swiss Chocolatier (European Tycoons #3)
Coming soon!
The Italian Winemaker (European Tycoons #4)
Coming soon!

Also by Leanne Lovegrove

Leanne's other novels:

Unexpected Delivery

Illegal Love

Keeper of the Light

A Good Life

Her Outback Home

Bellethorpe Series:

Love In Between (novella #1)

Caught In Between (novella #2)

Bellethorpe In Between Boxset (novellas #1 and #2)

Buried In Between novel #4

Novellas

Escapades of a Personal Stylist

Love on the Sweeping Plains

Anthologies

Love in a Sunburnt Land Vol 1

Love in a Sunburnt Land Vol 2